Rob Simson was a retired geography teacher and outdoor education leader with a background of professional writing in geographical and outdoor education, and a high school principal. He had an arts degree from University of Queensland and an MSc in environmental science from Griffith University. He had two self-published novels, one with Boolarong Press and one with Strictly Literary, and had also published a spiritual memoir with Smashwords entitled *To & From God.*

He passed away in 2018.

To the teachers of geography and lovers of quality teaching in the outdoors.

"Good teachers are the nutritionists of the mind."

– Robin Simson, 2009
(printed in award-winning soapbox article reproduced in Scope, the journal of the Fellowship of Australian Writers, Queensland).

Rob Simson

THE MEANING OF STREUTH

AUSTIN MACAULEY PUBLISHERS™
LONDON • CAMBRIDGE • NEW YORK • SHARJAH

Ordering Information
Quantity sales: Special discounts are available on quantity purchases by corporations, associations, and others. For details, contact the publisher at the address below.

Publisher's Cataloging-in-Publication data
Simson, Rob
The Meaning of Streuth

ISBN 9781641828307 (Paperback)
ISBN 9781641828314 (Hardback)
ISBN 9781645366201 (ePub e-book)

Library of Congress Control Number: 2019907912

www.austinmacauley.com/us

First Published (2021)
Austin Macauley Publishers LLC
40 Wall Street, 33rd Floor, Suite 3302
New York, NY 10005
USA

mail-usa@austinmacauley.com
+1 (646) 5125767

I would like to acknowledge the support of my family and encouragement of friends, Juliana de Nooey and Bronwyn Menkens. I would also like to thank the team at Austin Macauley for their belief in my work and persisting when they knew I was dying of bone cancer and would not be able to help with the promotion of the novel.

Chapter 1
Streuth

Friday, 12 August 2016

'Streuth!' It was a familiar response. He had inherited it—not genetically but as a meme handed down from his father. A way of thinking rather than an exclamation of wonder. Andrew remembered how his father's call would blurt out from a seat in the courtside stand. It was spontaneous. It was loud. Disturbing. Unhelpful. It happened when he hit a backhand passing shot down the line or scooped up an awkward half-volley to have it somehow hit the net cord and drop on the other side, unplayable!

Gary Thomas had been Andrew's coach and biggest fan. An outstanding junior himself at 12, another Rod Laver coming out of Central Queensland—promise, some said, of becoming as good as the 'Rocket'. And to boot there was the Goolagong factor—Aboriginal blood. His grandmother was a Garingbal woman. But Gary had never made the big time, he was never good enough to win through several rounds at the leading tournaments that paid prizemoney. Rather, Gary Thomas ended up making his living as a part-time tennis coach while changing direction to undertake an environmental science degree and becoming a National Park Ranger. His job didn't pay well, but it suited him as there was little other work for one with his qualifications, while the love of the outdoors and the Australian bush was inbred in him. Andy could still envisage his father shouting 'Streuth!' at tennis tournaments upon seeing a young aboriginal kid who had the hand-eye coordination, the commitment and the energy to go places in the tennis world.

In his late teens, Andrew Thomas realised, like his father before him, that he would never make it on the professional circuit, deciding his love of his ideals about teaching, being a nutritionist for kids' minds, was to be more important to him than his tennis. Yes, he would keep playing well and would enjoy the game; good enough to make the finals in those small tournaments held in Queensland country towns, yet never serious enough to be stressed if he lost. Back while still a top performing junior, some of his young rivals had nicknamed Andrew, 'Streuth', because they heard the cry so often while Andrew was playing. It was never, 'Great shot!', or 'Well done, boy!' that came from Gary Thomas's lips. 'Streuth!' for an ace. 'Streuth!' for a crosscourt off-forehand winner. 'Streuth!' for a slam-dunk overhead, even before the smashed ball landed either inside or outside the opponent's backline.

So it was 'Streuth!' that lit up in Andrew's mind when he saw her outside Gwen Lambert's hair salon, the sunlight bouncing off her long dark hair. The long tresses dancing around her shoulders, the peculiar shake of her head from left to right, and then a backwards tilt as her left hand stroked the dangling strands—a subconscious routine like a nervous tick. He was sure he knew that mannerism from somewhere, that particular style of announcing herself. So who was this beauty, and why was she in Rainworth Downs?

Monday, 15 August 2016

At the Rainworth Downs school gate, Guy Lambert shouted at Andrew, “Have you seen her, Sir, the new filly in town? Great catch for you, Sir!”

He was bold and loud-mouthed, young Guy, one of Andrew’s Grade 10 geography class. Not a great scholar, yet clever, quick-witted, with a reputation as a flashy rugby league player, and a growing notoriety as an off-the-rails underaged drinker and troublemaker. Indeed, Guy was a problem for his mother. Gwen Lambert lived the uncomfortable life of a widowed sole-parent with two younger girls to raise in addition to Guy. Her brother, a successful farmer and shire counsellor, had set her up in business after Guy’s father had been killed in a buck-jumping fall at the Emerald rodeo. She was popular and respected, but Guy was threatening all that.

Andrew smiled but pretended he didn’t hear. He walked quickly onto the old building that housed the English and Social Science staff room. On another day, another topic, Andrew would have admonished Guy. *Careful what you say, Lambert, your mother expects better from you! We all do! Finished your geography task work? I know, another pathetic excuse! It better be good! See you in class!*

Guy liked Mister Thomas and looked forward to the geography classes like he looked forward to physical education sessions or playing rugby league. ‘Sir’, he realised, was the one teacher who understood his need—a need he could not articulate but was there nagging at him. The need for a male authority figure in his life. Guy was also perceptive enough to know that Andrew Thomas was, in many ways, a misfit in Rainworth Downs. His favourite teacher did not play rugby league, did not drink at the Railway Tavern or the Comet Hotel, did not smoke, did not ride a horse or motorbike, and preferred playing tennis on Saturdays and going hiking alone in the nearby Carnarvon Ranges on Sundays to any other recreational pursuits. In geography class, there were repeated references to environmental issues and sustainability. His teacher's opposition to proposed new coal mines and the fracking process for coal-seam gas did not win Andrew Thomas friends except with the few descendants of the local Kongabula or Garingbal aboriginal clans who were fighting a 'land rights' battle with the Australian Government, or the one or two graziers whose leases would be terminated if the mines received government approval. The town was divided, as much as ten to one in favour of the mines. More work! More business! Those Greenies are absurd ratbags!

Cassandra Alvos, the new female clerk in the National Bank, wondered how she could ever fit in at Rainworth Downs. The bank had found her accommodation with Mister and Misses Bleakley, both in their 70s and, at times, just bordering on doddery. But they were respected. They had connections. The Bleakleys had both been schoolteachers in Rainworth and had decided to stay when they retired rather than make the sea change to Yeppoon, on the coast outside Rockhampton, as many elderly locals did. Rainworth Downs, more often simply Rainworth, was home. They had transitioned to be the caretakers at 'The Gregory Blockhouse'—a heritage site outside the town. They were experts on the history—the indigenous tribes of the area, the aboriginal art sites, the explorations of Ludwig Leichhardt and Major Thomas Mitchell; also A.C. Gregory, Queensland Surveyor-General, and claimant of the first of the early pastoral leases in the area. Then, the story of the massacre of the Wills family at Cullin-La-Ringo, the tales about the bush-ranging Kenniff Brothers; the Mulvany anthropological dig in the 1960s at Kenniff Cave, proving 19,000 years of occupation; the research of the art sites in the ranges by Grahame Walsh and the Walsh memorial in Injune. Cassie would learn, you couldn't escape the history at Rainworth Downs, the small town not far from where the Dawson Highway crossed the Comet River.

Cassie knew full well why she had undertaken the move to Rainworth Downs. It was a quiet town, away from the press. Away from the stalking. Away from the drama of all that. Her attempted suicide. How she'd tied weights to her body and plunged into the Fitzroy. It was dramatic, yes! Successful, no! She had been caught in the mud along the riverbank and rescued. Something about the strength of the incoming tide. She had lost consciousness and came to in hospital, with her mother and older sister by her side. She was bruised and battered, but alive. It was not a relief, this consciousness that would continue to bring back the memories she wished to bury. She still needed to find peace in being alive. She had no cause for celebration.

Marg Bleakley had been 'quietly informed' by Joseph Smithson, the National Bank manager. He was a prominent member of the Rainworth Catholic Congregation and flaunted it in the pursuit of business. He had called two days before Cassandra Alvos had arrived by train. She had listened intently to Joseph's pronouncement and agreed to be discrete. Marg believed she herself would not pry, but she knew what the town was like. She resolved that she simply wanted to help Cassandra fit in and be accepted. When you weren't local, born and bred around the Comet, you were an outsider, an intruder.

"What are your interests?" Marg asked over breakfast on the first morning at the old farmhouse near 'The Gregory Blockhouse'—the stone building. Marg and Fred had told her that the building had been the Rainworth Station food and equipment store back in the 1860s and 1870s, and now was a famous relic of a past era. Nothing like it had survived elsewhere in the country.

Cassie looked into a rugged friendly face, with the gray hair, soft smile, and a hint of concern in the voice. What did she know? This Misses Bleakley. Had she read the Rockhampton press? Had she suspected something of a cover-up?

Cassie hesitated, cautious with the words. "Photography and art, I guess. I loved art at school." It was simply an idea she was formulating. She hadn't thought it through. Her older sister, Alana, had sent her forth with a new digital Nikon. Alana would be disappointed if she didn't make use of it.

"There's lovely country, dearie, around here. In the ranges, the national parks. I used to walk up to Virgin Rock before the road was built. Wonderful views up there. We know someone who might like to show you around. Don't we, Fred?"

"Don't rush things," Fred replied, clambering to his feet and winking at Cassie. "Give the young lady time to get to know us, know a bit about the town." Then, by the back door, "I'll go and feed the chooks, and check on the eggs." An apology as such, leaving them to women's business.

"Any sport?" Marg went on with Fred out of earshot. "It's a sporty town. The footy and netball teams are called *'The Comets'*."

Cassie gulped, spilling her orange juice and grabbing a paper towel to soak up the mess. "Sorry. I'm not usually that careless," rushing on to cover the embarrassment. "I see there is a tennis centre with three courts. I used to play, way back, as a kid. Might have the courage to take it up again."

Courage? Marg mulled over the word. Was it courage to put aside the mental depression and suicide attempt, or was there something else, some mystery not yet to be revealed. Some passion, perhaps, that had produced its own sting.

"Well," Marg said, "I know someone who'd help get you back on the court. I feel sure. The same young man, Streuth— that's his nickname—he could also take you bushwalking. See our spectacular ranges…the lookouts and the aboriginal sites."

And with hardly a breath, Marg went on in her busy style. "Eat up! Enjoy your eggs. Farm fresh. Laid yesterday…And the bed? Oh dear, I didn't ask about the bed? Was it comfortable? Were you warm enough? The room? Will it do? Do you have enough storage, you know, for your clothes and your underthings? Let me know if you need any washing done. And, oh, did I say there's a steam iron and ironing board in the laundry. Feel free to use them.

And, by the way, do you have hiking boots, they could be useful…" continuing till Cassie got up to leave and prepare for her first day at work in the town.

She was sweet, Misses. Bleakley, Cassie thought, *like having a grandmother fussing around. But I will need to keep my own thoughts private...and my past...at least as much as I can hide without being rude.*

Cassandra knew she must let her family know about the Bleakleys…where she was staying. The room. The meals. Answering questions like Marg's, with her mother and sister in Rocky, listening together on the speaker phone. She would wait a few days. A week maybe. She wouldn't use Skype. Didn't want them reading any stress on her face. She wanted as much anonymity as possible. A low profile at least. She felt she couldn't trust her own mother, Lorae, what she might spill while speaking on the phone to Marg Bleakley. She shuddered. It was a worry.

Tuesday, 16 August 2016

The geography class filed in after the morning break. Guy Lambert and his mate, Seb, the aboriginal boy, the last as usual. Andy Thomas waited for them to settle, demanding attention.

"We're starting a new project today, it will run for the next five weeks, till the September holidays. Your efforts will count towards your end of year result. So get involved. Play your part."

Andrew Thomas paused, looking into the eyes of each of his ten students to make sure they were listening—front row, middle rows, back row. "You too, Jonathan, your role will be very important. We need your computer skills. You're savvy with the web, searching skills." It was a way of phishing for his attention, his cooperation—Jonathan Smithson, son of the National Bank Manager. "You will be working in teams during the project."

"What's this all about, Sir?" Guy Lambert blurted out, ignoring any rule of being invited to speak.

"Just listen, Guy!" The piercing look shutting him up. "I want you all to assume that an announcement has been made in Brisbane that a new dam is being planned for the Comet River, upstream from Rainworth Downs, to improve the security of the water supply for the town, and to guarantee the water that will be needed for the proposed additional coal mines in the Comet Basin area. You are to assume it's an important infrastructure project for the State of Queensland and will provide over 300 jobs in the area during the construction phase."

"Yes, Skye?" She had raised her hand in the back row. Skye Mattingley was his top student, the self-appointed leader of the girls' school, and the school captain. Not just a good scholar and stunningly attractive for her age, but an all-round sportswoman as well. She excelled on the netball and basketball courts, and also played tennis most Saturday afternoons, dragged along by her mother, the tennis club captain.

"What has that got to do with us? With geography? It's just politics!" And an echoing rumble accompanied by faint giggles flowed around the room. "A distraction from the real issues, like climate change and world population overload."

"Let's think about it, Skye. We need a sustainable water supply and a recreation area closer than the coast would be very popular. Without knowing all the details, how many of you would be in favour of a new dam?"

"Good for fishing and swimming!" It was Seb Goodman, his animated face, broad nose, and heavy lips, displaying his ancestry.

Other comments followed around the room:

"Like that one near Emerald, Lake Fairbairn. We go there for picnics." It was Grace.

"Water from that dam irrigates my Uncle Reg's cotton farm," said Jane.

"It's also supposed to stop flooding in Emerald, but it didn't in 2011," said Skye.

"Who's going to pay for this dam? Malcolm what's 'is name—the PM guy. He's rolling in dosh?" asked typical Guy.

"Whose land will be resumed? Another land grab like the last one for the mines?" said Danielle.

"That's Joe Adams, my cousin's land, that was taken!" said Jenny.

"It might create jobs. Good for the pubs," said Seb.

"Well, let's have a vote," Andrew said, establishing control again. "You might change your minds later if we do a thorough investigation of the value and implications of a new dam. That's what geographers do. Bring together all the facts from all the different sources. But just now, before we get started, do you think we should have a new dam or we shouldn't?"

A few cautious hands went up. Andrew realised the students could be suspecting his own position—that he was against dams. Against destroying nature. They might even know he was a supporter of the Wilderness Society and the Environmental Defenders. Round the town, they understood he was known as a 'Bloody Greenie' and opposed to the new coal mines.

"Okay, we'll have a secret ballot. No one else needs to know how you vote. We'll do it first thing in tomorrow's class. It will be a simple ballot to fill in. Just *'yes'* or *'no'*. I have prepared a handout, explaining the class project for you to take home. As homework, you could discuss the issue with your parents, but make up your own minds when we have done our investigation. Make sure your parents understand it is just an exercise, a simulation. It's not for real. It's designed to make you think about the issue and question, to do what geographers do. Question. Question. Question. Not make hasty decisions."

Wednesday, 16 August 2016

She rose from the enquiry counter, coming forward to welcome him into the bank. "How can I help you, Sir?"

Again, there was something familiar about her, but he couldn't place it. The deep brown eyes, whitened teeth, broad smile, red-brown lipstick, and even the voice from somewhere in the past, recalled like a faint bellbird song coming from a distance. Yet she didn't give anything away. Didn't show any recognition, just tossed her hair around and radiated beauty.

Another 'Streuth' moment. The excitement started in his stomach, surging up with a sudden rush to his face and spilling out crimson. "I…I should draw some money out. Yes, almost forgot."

"Then Claudia will look after you, over at the teller's counter. Mister…?" she responded.

"Thomas, Andrew Thomas," he replied, not moving, not wanting to miss anything she might say. Any other mannerisms. The touch of an earring. The way she held a pen. Things to remember. To build on first impressions. To treasure.

"Then you must be the one and only Streuth?" she smiled.

"Yes, I'm called that. That stupid name! I prefer Andy…with friends."

"Andy," she mouthed, locking it in her memory.

"And you might be Cassandra? Welcome to Comet River country."

"Why, thank you." There was a smile and the hint of a chuckle. He smiled back. Then, as she turned and went to her desk, he was rewarded—the accentuated bum curve trapped in a tight navy skirt, delighting him.

Cassie felt it immediately. She liked him. Liked his easiness. Bright hazel eyes. Curly brown hair tied back pigtail fashion, like a young Roger Federer. His athletic manliness and tidy casual dress. But he was not spectacularly handsome. His Aryan countenance carried a blemish or two—a small birthmark across the right temple, and what she assumed were some chicken pox scars on the left cheek.

Immediately her mind raced on: What a contrast to the stiff and pedantic Mister Smithson who had inducted her into all the aspects of her role as the third staff member at the bank. The technology they were using. The online banking system. The important accounts. The major customers she should get to know. Business people. Demanding clients. Hopefully, there were more men like Andy in the town. Pleasant natured and unattached? Approachable? Understanding? And what about the inquisitiveness behind this Andy Thomas's eyes? Was he here in the bank on purpose to pry? Had Marg Bleakley been speaking to him? What had she said? What might he already know?

Eventually, as his left hand wiped the side of his sweating neck, he moved away, feeling scrutinised, while hoping nothing would show, his arousal in his trousers. At the teller counter he drew his money out. Claudia Grant, he understood, was a true local, born in the town and mother of Jenny in his English and geography classes. She nonchalantly counted the money out in fifty-dollar notes. \$50, \$100, \$150, \$200. It was money he accepted but didn't really need, since he paid almost everything by card.

"She's nice, isn't she," Claudia whispered and winked as he put the \$200 away in his wallet.

He turned back and stood a moment looking towards Cassandra, and then remembering his real mission. "Miss…?" Realising he didn't yet know her family name. "Misses. Bleakley, said you might like to play tennis." He saw her grin. Now she understood it had never been a chance encounter. "I assume you know where the courts are. 1:30 Saturday. Hope to see you there."

"The name's Cassie, Cassandra Avos," she called back as the automatic door opened for him.

"Right." He nodded back, then politely left. Feeling foolish. He rubbed a finger across the birthmark on his temple. Did she notice it?

Chapter 2

Thursday, 17 August 2016

"Mister James has kindly counted the votes for us. Six to four in favour of the dam being built. What do you think of that, Guy?" It was the Thursday geography lesson and the class was quickly aware that Sir was in a particularly buoyant mood.

"Ask Seb. He says his people will be against it. Doesn't want to speak up, though. It's Kongabula land, he says, that Nuga Nuga area upstream." Seb Goodman gave Guy a high-five. Smiling as if to add in jest, '*My country. White fella leave it be.*'

"Sir," it was Jenny Grant waving her left arm around—left-handed and proud of it. Curly haired, pale-faced, Jenny was always pleased when she could contribute anything, as long as it sounded intelligent, that got her noticed. Trying hard to compete with Skye. "Could we go out to have a look? Another field trip like we did with our history study of 'The Gregory Blockhouse'. Go to where the Comet Weir is? And Lake Nuga Nuga. Is that where this dam would go?"

Andrew Thomas was equally pleased. Jenny's suggestion would help engage the class. It may have come from her mother, Claudia, but any parent support was helpful. He would need the principal's approval, and one of the local school feeder buses, but it was part of his forward plan anyway.

"Good suggestion, Jenny. Maybe we could get Skye's dad, the shire engineer, to come along and explain some things, and also Mister Smallbone, the CEO from the Regional Council's office in the town."

"Sir?" It was Jonathan Smithson, gaining attention as all the class turned their heads and starred at him, amazed. Jonathan didn't often speak up in class. A loner most of the time, embarrassed by the braces on his teeth, his spectacles and his pimpled face. "We need to consult a geologist and a hydrologist and look up information on other dams."

"Thanks, Jonathan, more good thinking." Andy Thomas, realising from the confused looks that he would need to explain why the input from both those professions was crucial to their investigation. As he wrote both words on the electronic whiteboard, he added comments. "Geologist, of course, one who studies rocks, their mineral composition, and properties. Hydrologists study climate and river flow and make predictions about water yield for town supplies, irrigation, and industry. The importance of both should become more apparent as you investigate further."

He gave the students time to make some notes, then went on, "Before we go any further with this, I am dividing the class into three teams. Four in the *'against the dam'* group as per our ballot numbers, and the rest divided up into the *'pro-dam group'* led by Jenny and a small research group, those with good computer research skills, led by Jonathan."

There was a flurry of semi-audible groans and a few cheers.

"Who's the foolish emu leading the *'against group'*?" It was Guy—irrepressible again.

"Not you, Guy, I'm separating you and Seb. Seb can help Skye with the indigenous perspective, attitudes opposed to taming the river."

"Sir," Skye jumped to her feet in protest. "But I'm all for the dam. It would be great for the town."

"A good reason, Skye, to have you in the other camp. Finding the facts that prove it may not be sensible to dam the Comet. Forcing you to think about another point of view. Like in a formal debate."

"But I want—"

"No, Skye!" Andrew cut her off. "Pleading will not work with me. This is a class simulation exercise. It's not for real, but we are going to play it that way. Take the role of becoming well-informed responsible citizens. Some for the dam proposals, some against. This is a meaningful inquiry and we must approach it as good geographers with an open mind."

Skye was no more successful pleading with her mother. "Your brother is at boarding school, and we are not leaving you at home alone."

Skye pulled violently on her long blonde hair and screwed her face into her most surly look with her tongue poking from the side of her mouth. Her mother ignored it. She was used to the teenager's dramatics. She had some sympathy for Skye since she had been dragged along to the

May meeting of The Blockhouse Committee, but was never once given an invite to speak. She feared Skye would feel out of place and put down again. She wanted her daughter and other teenagers to have a chance to contribute. It was their town after all, and being undervalued and disheartened was a sure reason for them to escape as soon as they could.

"Marg Bleakley is preparing dinner for us all. As well as your dad and I, Mister James and Mister Smallbone will be there with their wives. And the Bleakleys have a new boarder, Cassie somebody, Marg wants us to meet."

"Alvos, Cassie Alvos, Mum. She's working with Jenny's mum at the National Bank. They say she's glamorous, but a bit strange. Not likely to fit in around here."

Over at the dinner at the Bleakleys, Skye Mattingley found herself excused by her mother to find something to do with Cassie Alvos to pass the time while the formal meeting took place. She sat on the floor in Cassie's room examining a scrapbook she'd picked off a shelf. It had opened at a page with a photo of Cassandra with a tennis trophy that caught her eye. Cassie looked young, perhaps 12 or 13, wearing a cap backwards like a young Leyton Hewitt. There was no caption.

"You must have been a good player to win a championship trophy. Does it say Under 14 Queensland Champion? My mum would like me to be that good, but I'm not. Do you still play?"

"No! Gave it away soon after that was taken," Cassie responded, looking away, not wanting to engage.

"Why? Didn't you miss it?" Skye continued.

Cassie was even slower to answer. "I had a fall off a mountain bike and broke my right wrist and tibia very badly. Couldn't get back on the court for six months. Took up surfing for a while."

"If you like the surf, why are you here? Why not the Yeppoon coast? Or better still, Noosa or the Gold Coast?"

"That's how it is. I'm here for work." The answer needed to be blunt. Cassandra didn't want this inquisitiveness to go on directed at herself. "Your mother, Penny, approached me before dinner about playing tennis again, but I don't have a racquet or tennis dress."

"Do come. Mum would be so pleased. We need extra players to keep the club going."

"Mister Thomas also asked me. Claudia, at the bank, said Mister Thomas is one of your teachers? What's he like other than being a keen tennis player?"

"He's cool. Popular. He teaches geography, history, and English. We have just started this geography project. It's already stirred up the town. Have you heard about it yet?"

"Claudia said something about it today. About a proposed dam on the Comet River. Her daughter must be in the class with you?"

"Yes, and Mister Smithson's son, Jonathan. He's a nerd. A computer games fanatic."

"You sound like you don't like Jonathan. If the project, I understand, is a simulation exercise, gathering relevant information, Jonathan Smithson's technology skills could be very useful. Researching things about dams. How the water could be used."

Skye sniffed and screwed up her nose. "So Sir is saying. He's clever, Sir, the way he's sucking Jonathan in. Getting him do some geography work disguised as IT."

There was something in the manner of Skye's responses. A delight in her voice speaking about Andy Thomas, but now it was she who was all the time looking away, avoiding eye contact. Was there a schoolgirl crush? Or was Andy 'gay', perhaps, and Skye knew it.

"Well, your Sir, Mister Thomas, if you're right about his abilities, should I trust him?"

Skye was mystified by the tone and implications of the question. *Maybe*, she thought, *this was why I was told that Cassandra Alvos was a bit weird.* Some things Cassie wanted kept secret also kept her nervous and wary. Her poise was just a show.

"I'm not sure. Several of the girls idolise him, like he's a pop star. Silly how they pretend to be… *'available'*. But he makes it abundantly clear he doesn't want any advances. Is that what you want to know? Not from the female teachers, either. Around the town they call him *'Streuth'* I don't know where that comes from, but I'd be surprised if it was a rude putdown—at least, how it started."

"Maybe I'll find out someday," Cassie said. "Think I hear your father calling. Must be time to go. Nice meeting you, Skye." *This was enough exposure for one week,* she thought.

As they were gathered at the cars, preparing to leave, Les Smallbone asked Skye if she was in the class involved in the study about a dam on the Comet he was hearing about.

"Yes," she replied politely, "Mister Thomas is my geography teacher."

“And you know it’s *‘fake’* news, don’t you!” It was a demand, not a question. “Such an idea was dismissed over a decade ago. Mister Thomas is stirring up an old conflict. The town was divided on the issue back then. We’ll have neighbours arguing all over again. Fights in the street. Can’t he teach his subject out of books? That’s the way I learned!”

The CEO of the shire office was a small balding man with a pronounced stoop. He and his wife were friendly with her parents, and theoretically, he was her father’s boss, but that didn’t mean, in her mind, that she had to like him. Skye felt she needed to defend her favourite teacher, but all she could do was pant her distress. Words wouldn’t come.

“Easy, Les.” Gareth Mattingley was interjecting. “It’s just a simulation exercise, making the work in geography seem realistic, have some purpose. I believe lots of half-truths gained traction back in the 90s, before kids like Skye were born. Knowing Andy Thomas, he will encourage open minds and a thorough investigation of the pros and cons of the imagined dam.”

“It’s much easier now,” Penny Mattingley added. “The students will be able to find reports on the web—geology, engineering feasibility, rainfall, and streamflow figures, even anthropological data. I think it’s a great challenge for them to research like that and reach decisions based on knowledge, not sentiment.”

“That may be. But the same conflicting arguments will surface,” Les Smallbone shot back while hastily scrambling into his car to leave. “Don’t forget St. Matthew’s Day ’98!”

“Interesting,” Fred Bleakley said while holding Marg firmly around the waste. “That’s not your worry, Skye, that old history. Marg and I can help your class if it’s needed with what we know from back then. The dam proposal in the 1990s. Goodnight everyone. Safe driving."

Skye noted that Mister James, the school principal, and his wife had remained silent except for saying goodbye and thanking Marg for the dinner.

Saturday, 20 August 2016

It was four-love when she protested that that was enough. Cassie was short of breath; her legs and right arm muscles were aching. It had been ten years after all, though she wasn't explaining that to anyone. She had just gone to the tennis club to watch and be friendly, but Penny Mattingley had persuaded her to have a little hit up with Andy, while eight club members were playing doubles on the other two courts. She kept protesting that she didn't have tennis shoes or a racquet, and her slacks and floral top were hardly tennis gear. It had no effect. They were persistent till she gave in.

"Here, take my racquet," Skye had said. "I'm sitting off. Helping mum with the afternoon tea."

Cassie found that her Adidas sneakers were okay on the synthetic court, but the slacks were hot and restrictive. She wished she'd worn shorts. It was so awkward, so unfamiliar at first, till after ten minutes of hitting up she felt stronger. Some of the old rhythm was still there. She realised that Andy was impressed. Imagined him thinking, *this woman is more than a beautiful face and curvy body. She is really capable, alert, and quick. A good forehand plus both power and finesse with her double-handed backhand.*

For the fun of it, she challenged him to a match where she knew he'd enjoy outplaying her, showing off some of his own flare. She had trouble with the service games, missing first serves and finding her weak second serve easily dispatched for winners; yet when receiving, she did better. In the fourth game, she beat Andy with a toss over his head as he rushed the net, and then hit him in the chest with fierce backhand drive as he approached the net again. Penny and Skye were cheering, she remembered, after she got back to the Bleakleys and told the story to Marg and Fred. "That's when I'd bent over in a fit of laughter. The game had gone to deuce before Andy hit the winner."

There was a toilet and shower for tourist use in 'The Gregory Blockhouse' building, 60 metres away from the Bleakley's cottage. With their agreement, Cassie preferred to use it rather than the shared bathroom in the house. Under the warm shower, she contemplated. *I'm already in a flutter over Andy Thomas. Here I am pleasing myself, thinking of him. He's handsome. Carefree. Fun-loving. An adored teacher 'You're already a smash hit with Mister Thomas!' Skye had said. For sure, Skye was jealous. Poor dear. She's a clever girl. Bright and honest and Andy obviously encourages her scholarship. I hope he knows to keep it strictly as a student-teacher relationship. Nothing more. I didn't come to 'Comet Country' for a romance. I wanted escape. Peace and quiet. Anonymity. Marg might already think she can be a matchmaker. Fred said to me, 'Beware, she is the local wedding celebrant.' Apparently, non-church weddings sometimes took place in the gardens Fred maintains around The Blockhouse.*

Chapter 3

Monday, 21 August 2016

"Ah, Mister Thomas, Andy. Just needed a word with you before class. Come into my office and shut the door."

Andy complied with the request but wondered at the concern in the principal's voice. Douglas James was a good principal, in his second year at the school. He was determined to set high standards for the staff and students. Because of a lingering inferiority complex that dated back to the disadvantage of having been born with a hair lip and still bearing a noticeable scar on his upper lip, he was often indecisive and cautious in decision-making. He spoke with the hint of a lisp.

"We may have a problem with this project of yours. Apparently, there was a study regarding a dam on the Comet River done in the 1990s, and the proposal back then got shelved."

"Well, I knew that, Sir. It was almost 20 years ago, well before either of us was in this town. But I knew when I planned the activity that there are documented reports. I want the students to find that out for themselves. Jonathan Smithson will be in his element, chasing them up on the web. Rainfall, stream flow, environmental impact reports.

And the other students will follow his lead. It is a real geographical search for them. Bringing together relevant information from many sources—scientific, economic, and social."

"Unfortunately, the proposal back then led to some serious conflict in this town. There was some kind of violent brawl on St. Matthew's Day, 18 August 1998. Les Smallbone, do you know him, from the Regional Council, mentioned that when I was coming away from the 'The Gregory Blockhouse' committee meeting on Friday night."

"1998? That's before our students were born."

"Yes, I realise that. But in a small country town, there will almost certainly be those still bearing grudges over what happened. Stories will have passed down through families. This project could stir up old sores. That could give us a bad name—you, me, the school!"

"But, Sir, it is such an excellent opportunity for this class. It's designed to make the subject of geography come alive. Not just book study and memory work. Real enquiry learning. Learning because they have suddenly found a desire to know. I've been planning this for months. Come to the class later in the week and see how they are engaged."

That morning, Doug James had felt he should call the project off. Now, he was in two minds. *Andy Thomas is a good teacher—one of, if not the best, on my staff. I don't want to begrudge Andy the opportunity to be innovative. He represents a new breed. New pedagogy. He can show the other staff the way forward in the IT age. The younger teachers on the staff would support him. But dare I ignore, there could be serious consequences. Parent's complaints.*

Indigenous elders' complaints. Even an Education Departmental enquiry.

Andy felt the tension. He could see Mister James was procrastinating. Unsure. Nervous. But finally, his school principal delivered what Andy hoped he'd hear.

"Well, two things. Tell the students to keep their parents and relatives out of it for now. Keep things tightly within class. And advertise your field excursion as something else. Geology and landforms, or irrigation schemes. Don't link the outing directly to your *'Fake News'* study, as Smallbone called it, or anything directly to do with coal mining."

"You mean, let the students draw those inferences."

"Yes, a subtle approach, if you will," Doug James responded while slapping his forehead, hoping like hell he wasn't being a fool with this decision.

In class, the geography students were in workshop mode, the groups discussing the approaches they could take to gathering information relevant to the project. Andy played some soft environmental music while they worked. It helped set the tone without disrupting concentration.

"Sir," an excited call from Jonathan Smithson. "There's a report I've found on the Comet Dam proposal. Dated 1997. Looks like a book was written about it? It's not in the town library. I've already checked. Would we be able to locate a copy?"

Andy Thomas's face lit up. He'd hoped the students would uncover the information available about the 1990s investigation. He didn't want to do too much of the leading. That would defeat the purpose of the dam proposal exercise.

"Where might there be a copy? Jonathan? Who would have it?"

Jonathan was struggling to give an answer, so Skye, as usual, was quick to speak up. "The State Library. State Department of Resources. The Shire Office."

"And there's a local history library at 'The Gregory Blockhouse'," Guy added, knowing himself that he was not just the class clown.

"Full marks, the three of you. Now you'll have to do a hunt, that's part of the task, but try to keep your parents out of this. You are the student investigators. You have till Tuesday's class to come up with your group strategy reports. Now, for a geomorphology lesson."

He had prepared a diagram which he handed out and projected on the electronic whiteboard as he spoke. It showed a geological cross-section, to explain the relationship of the local rock types and the resulting landforms, layer upon layer, the tertiary basalts on top.

Skye was making copious notes and annotated the printed diagram. She could see Jenny Grant and some of her team doing the same, so she was determined to be thorough.

Stratigraphy, that was a new word…surely for all the class, except, perhaps, Jonathan. It had to do with the layers of sedimentary rocks exposed under the basalts, different formations—another new word, how it was being used. Some formations were permeable, letting water pass through into underground reservoirs and then the water could seep out in another place, even hundreds of kilometres away from the intake area. Everyone heard about the Precipice Sandstone forming the cliffs when they visited Carnarvon Gorge. Now, there were other names—Clematis Sandstone, Mooloyember Mudstones, conglomerates, and shales. Some with coal seams and possible sites for gas extraction.

She remembered the science teacher in Grade 8, explaining that the top layer of the Consuelo Tableland above Carnarvon Gorge in the Carnarvon National Park was composed of basalt solidified from lava flows during eruptions. The lava had spread over an enormous area in a sheet and covered the older rock layers Sir was talking about. It still capped the older rocks in many places. Sir was giving hints, she realised, that might explain where to build a dam and how successful it would be. She feared, she might need to explain it all again to Seb, Grace, and Dannielle in her team. Things she would follow up on the internet at home.

Saturday, 27 August 2016

Cassie was on the court in a women's doubles match when the rain started. It was blowing in from the west, a scudding storm but enough to wet the courts so more play was impossible. She had bought a second-hand bicycle arranged for her by Gwen Lambert, and now could travel around Rainworth Downs without being dependent on lifts from Fred Bleakley or Claudia.

"Sorry, tennis is over for the day. Even if the rain stops, the courts will take an hour or two to dry." Andy explained what was the obvious as the other players were picking up their gear and rushing out to their cars.

"I came by bike. I'll wait here till the rain passes." Cassie told him.

"I'll wait with you." Just the opportunity he wanted, touching her on the shoulder as she looked up at him. *Cassandra*...to himself.

"You needn't worry, I'll be fine." Her gorgeous brown eyes pleading something different.

"No. I'll stay!" And then grinning with delight, "Tell me about yourself. How come this beautiful woman has come into my life?" He would have winked but his facial muscles always failed to respond when he tried. Instead, he proffered a swoon to make her smile.

"I can't," she said meekly while putting a hand to her face, hiding a tear.

He quickly handed her a tissue from his tennis bag, wondering whether to push on and ask why.

"I have my reasons. I don't want to talk about it."

There is a secret, Andy thought as he went to make a cup of tea. He already knew that for some reason she disliked coffee, but that was trivia. There was so much more he desired to know. "I'm sorry, there is no milk. Penny has taken the milk home. Can you drink it black?"

Cassie nodded, composing herself.

He brought the tea, and they sat together, peering, searching, trying to delve into the hidden, their secret selves—but saying nothing.

"Do you have a girlfriend?" she asked, needing to break the silence.

"No, not till now." The implication was obvious as he took hold of her free hand. "I had a relationship that got quite serious while I was at university, but it didn't last. She wanted her freedom, so she said. She took up with a rugby player for a while, then returned home to help nurse a sick mother."

Cassie noted the *'she'*. That cleared up one concern.

The rain stopped almost as suddenly as it had started. She handed back the tea mug and got up. "I should go. In case there's another shower coming. Thanks, Andy, you are very kind."

He followed her out to the bicycle. Checking she was okay. "Would you come bushwalking with me tomorrow?" he asked, hesitantly. "In the National Park?"

"To Virgin Rock? Marg said it's spectacular."

"No," he replied, hoping she realised it was not a rebuff. "That's in the Minerva Hills. Acid volcanic country. I prefer the sandstone country, so dissected. Such interesting shapes and forms to photograph. Spring wildflowers galore. You'll see Mt. Mooloolong, my favourite rock pinnacle."

"Not sure," she said, turning away holding her bike tightly. "It might rain again."

Andy wasn't being put off. "I'll ring the Bleakley's tonight, to see if you've agreed to come. Do you have a good camera?" He added as she mounted.

"Yes."

"Then you won't regret it if you join me. You're in for a treat." His voice fading off as she rode away.

Skye Mattingley had played netball in the morning, a home game for the under 16 Comets against the Blackwater team. They'd lost 48–45, so she was not in a good mood. She had pleaded too much research to complete when asked to also go to tennis. She had found a plethora of information and illustrations about rock strata, folding, synclines, and anticlines, all somewhat teasing; but still couldn't figure out how the properties of the various rock layers affected the construction of a dam. She was still sitting in front of the family computer when her mother came home disgruntled.

"We were just into our second sets when the rain started. It hasn't rained for weeks, so why a storm to bugger things up on Saturday? Could have held off till this evening, then we'd have all cheered."

She flopped down on a chair beside Skye. Pictures and diagrams of rock cuttings occupied the screen. "What ya working on?"

"Research for the project Mister Thomas has us doing. All about sedimentary rock types in our local area. Was he there? At tennis?"

"Yes! And that Cassandra girl from the National Bank came again. She's surprisingly good. She and Andy beat me and Josh Gibson in the first set. We only won one game."

"Josh? That's Merle Gibson's son, the Bleakley's grandson. He's not such a great player. Can't volley very well because of how he holds the racquet. Did Cassie have her own racquet this time?"

"No, she borrowed one from Andy. It was a heavy men's racquet. Hits her backhand harder than her forehand, and she's quick at the net."

"Did she tell you she won the Queensland under 14 State Champs as a junior, then gave up playing soon after?"

"Well, that explains a lot. How did you find that out? She clams up when you ask anything about her family."

"Saw this photo of her with the trophy…in her bedroom, that night at the Bleakleys for 'The Gregory Blockhouse' meeting. I suspect there's something else she's not saying. She was weeping when she told me she'd had a bad bike accident, broke her arm and wrist. I think there's more to it than that, the way she was crying, hugging herself then tugging on her hair. In the photo, she had very short hair and a fringe. Thought to myself, she wanted to look like a boy."

"Well, a tough look and forceful shots might have been her winning strategy. I wonder who coached her back then?"

"Andy's dad is a part time tennis coach. Did you know that?"

"Yes, but Gary Thomas has coached in country towns like Roma, where he is now. It was probably a State Coach if she was that good."

But by the expression on her mother's face, Skye could tell something more was stirring her mind.

"What is it, Mum? What are you thinking?"

"Never you mind, young lady. Get on with your geography assignment," Penny frowned at Skye as she took her tennis bag and racquets to her bedroom.

Chapter 4

Sunday, 28 August 2016

Cassie was ready when Andy arrived at 6:30 a.m. She had dressed in blue jeans and a floral shirt. She held a broad-brimmed straw hat with a red band, her hair plaited, hanging down her back.

"Will this do?" she inquired, indicating her clothes and red sneakers as Andy jumped out of the green Suzuki Jimny and took the food basket Marg Bleakley had prepared for them both.

"You'd look stunning whatever you wear." Then added patting the top of his vehicle, "You'll see this old girl is very comfortable. Hop in, princess."

"I brought my camera."

"A Nikon Coolpix, no less. Should take some great photos, close ups and with the telephoto lens."

"A going away present from my sister," Cassie replied.

"Are you experienced in photography?'

"Mostly self-taught. When I was in Spain, the eldest of my male cousins, the leader of a surfing group, asked me to take shots of the guys riding the waves using his Pentax Spotmatic. That was pre-digital, with colour prints. I used his telephoto lens a good deal, and he was pleased with the results. Focus and depth of field were somewhat of a challenge. I'll be experimenting with the Nikon today."

"Well, let's get going. It's a long drive, about 90 minutes to where we're going in the Ka Ka Mundi section of the National Park. The strange name has aboriginal origins, I believe."

After they'd been going a while and she'd got used to the rough ride in the little 4WD, Cassie asked, "Speaking of strange names, how come you got the nickname, Streuth?"

So Andy told the story about his father calling out at tennis matches. Then, he added, "I had been in Rainworth Downs just over a year and went to Biloela with some other locals to play in a tennis tournament. Another guy I knew from Juniors called out to me, '*Hi, Streuth. Streuth! Fancy catching up with you out here!*' Then, the name came back to Rainworth as a sort of a punishment for being such a nice guy."

"So? Am I punishing you now, since you seem, to me, like a nice guy?" she inquired, looking towards him, and aching for him to glimpse back at her with a smile. "I don't wish to intentionally add to your torment."

"You know, I don't even know how I should spell it, the silly name. I can think of at least three ways— s, t, r, e, u, th…s, t, r, e, w, th, and s, t, r, double o, th."

"Well, I believe the spelling is just trivia. It's the sentiment of the speaker, and then more important, the personality behind the name, the receiver of the snarl or compliment that gives it meaning. Just as with written words, the themes explored behind the glossy book cover are what really count."

Andy drove on. Silent for a while, trying to comprehend and digest what Cassie had just said.

"So tell me about your name, Cassandra. And why *'Cassie'* and not *'Sandy'*?"

"My mother's idea, what I should use when I was coming out to Rainworth Downs."

"What should I make of that?" This time, taking his eyes off the road trying to see how she responded.

"Careful," she called as a cow and calf strayed onto the road in front.

He slowed immediately, to be sure to miss the animals. "Well?" And she could tell he smelt deception, confirmed when he repeated, "Is Cassandra not your real name?"

"Well, yes and no," she admitted shyly. "Maybe, I'll tell you, later. Not today."

After 50 minutes, they turned off the bitumen and headed south on a gravel road. At one spot, there was a large thimble-shaped sandstone hill and in the cultivated field, in the foreground, a flock of brolgas was feeding and frolicking where a sorghum crop had recently been harvested. Andy stopped the car so Cassie could get out and take some photos. It was a chance to play with her camera. Experience the value of the optical vibration reduction feature, her shots stabilised because of the high shutter speed; and the benefit of the electronic viewfinder, enabling her to carefully compose the photos as she zoomed in and adjusted the depth of field.

"Aren't they beautiful," she said, getting back into the car beside him. "I even captured some of them dancing using the video setting. Thank you for stopping."

"My pleasure. It's my delight to please a beautiful lady."

"Don't overdo it! You hardly know me."

When they had left behind the farmland and entered the woodland in the National Park, the flowers delighted Cassie even more. Wattles, splendid, but as Andy commented, mostly past their best; callistemons and leptospermums coming into bloom, flowering angophoras and eucalypts attracting flocks of parrots; and an occasional flame tree in a patch of dense scrub.

"Andy, look at those red grevilleas. They glow in the sunlight, like a flamenco costume."

"Yes," Andy replied, "They are special, an endemic species, and when I come here in spring those grevilleas, the mass displays of golden native peas, and the other heath plants in flower always amazes me."

When they reached a spot where the groundwater trickled out of the sandstone, forming clear water pools, Andy stopped and parked in the shade. "This is one of the many springs in the ranges. Take a look around. Great place to take more photographs."

Cassie was ecstatic. She kept snapping photos—water lilies, miniature waterfalls, Andy's reflection in the water. Always experimenting till she got the composition, focus, and lighting to her satisfaction. Eliminating those shots not just right in her mind.

"It's a native garden paradise," Cassie gushed with delight. "Thanks for bringing me here."

"The best is yet to come," Andy said in acknowledgment.

They took their lunch hamper and a rug from the back of the Suzuki and set off uphill through a cleft in a cliff and out on to a higher wildflower meadow. After strolling and taking more photos for an hour, they came out on a shelf, looking west into an eroded valley.

What a view Cassie thought. A domed-shaped hill honeycombed with little caves to their left, and a spectacular white sandstone tower off perhaps a kilometre to their right. "Cave Hill and Mt. Mooloolong," Andy named them. "The perfect spot to have lunch."

They sat down to enjoy the sandwiches, biscuits, and fruit Marg Bleakley had kindly provided.

"What's that sound, the whistling?" Cassie asked.

"Look up there, hovering. It's a whistling kite, *Haliastur sphenurus.* Listen, the song begins by descending down the scale, followed by an upscale piercing spike, then falls away again. It may be calling to a mate."

Andrew tried whistling like the bird. "Rather a poor imitation," Cassie laughed.

"I'm calling to you."

"If it's a love call, you failed."

Andrew gave a hurt look then changed the subject. "What I love is the aesthetics of this place—the juxtaposition of landform shapes and colours. The fantastic Mooloolong temple to our right, that striking Red Hill outcrop directly across the valley, and the dome of Cave Hill to our left. It's a brilliantly fine day, but here in the rain, or on a cloudy evening when the sun is setting, it is just as magical. Maybe that's what the kite sings about. The joy of being here."

"You're so passionate about the natural world, aren't you?"

"I try to tell my students they should fall in love with nature. Enjoy the environment in all of its moods."

"That's a romantic view. Life has some very bleak periods that can cause a lot of grief. Does not the bird call in anguish when its young are dying of starvation in a drought, or its mate has been shot by a human poacher?"

Andrew didn't have an answer. "Hold it, that look," she said, and grabbed up her camera to take him looking forlorn.

She stood up, tossed her plaited hair back, and put on her hat. Now, let's go to where I can get a good shot of Mt. Mooloolong with you in focus in the foreground. I will call it '*Andrew and his Bride'*."

That night, after she had showered and eaten, Cassie found the energy to tell the Bleakley's all about her wonderful day. Sitting on the bed in her small room, they insisted on seeing her photographs displayed on her desktop computer. Fred was quick to congratulate her. "Great images," he said, and she could see more than once how he wanted to clap.

Marg, as she had come to expect, was more interested in any hint of a blossoming romance. "The love dance of the Brolgas, I've only seen that once, myself. You were lucky. So good of Andy to stop for you."

When they left her room, sleep came easily to Cassandra. Any desire to further relive the highlights of the outing to the National Park or the feeling of pleasure at Andy's attentiveness, faded into nothingness. In the morning, she reflected. She hadn't slept so well since leaving that hospital bed in Rockhampton.

Monday, 29 August 2016

"Have you heard?" Jenny Grant shouted to Skye as she joined five Year 10 girls gathered in a huddle under the trees near the school gate. "The town's buzzing with it!"

"What?"

"That new sexy piece, works with Jenny's mother at the Bank," One of the group went on over a chorus of giggles.

"Cassie Alvos?" Skye queried.

"We don't know her name. But she's dating Mister Thomas. Seen driving out of town together yesterday morning and didn't return till after dark." More nods, faint whistles, and laughter.

"She acts like a catwalk model, strutting around town. All smart clothes, headbands, and dangling earrings."

"And platform heels. My mum thinks she's a moll!"

"My dad and Uncle Alan have been told they're not to go near the bank!"

And so it continued till Skye interjected.

"Have any of you even met her? Spoken to her?" The vague looks told her she was right. "Well, don't make judgments without knowing the facts. Gossip is hurtful and mostly exaggerated, if not untrue."

The outburst silenced them and Skye walked away smiling to herself. *Sir, Mister Thomas, had said, opinion based on hearsay isn't worth considering. You need to gather all the facts first. That was what the class was charged to do in the Comet Dam investigation.*

Marg Bleakley sat, waiting for her regular monthly trim at Gwen Lambert's hairdressing salon. It was the best place in Rainworth Downs to listen in on the local gossip. Fred would also be getting all the local stories, sitting in the bar at the railway. After her hair cut, she would join him there for a counter lunch. It had become a habit, this little outing, first Tuesday of the month.

Sally, the barmaid from The Comet Hotel was having her hair permed— '*the latest blond spiral style'*, whatever that was. Probably lots of curls to dangle around her ears and shoulders to the delight of her customers. Without seeing the face, Marg knew the guttural voice with its cadences and sharpness. The softer voice was Gina's, wife of an electrician working at the Pungana South coal mine. She was having a new *'short style'* cut like the poster on the wall. There was idle chatter, and then the talk turned to the new woman at the National Bank.

"I reckon she's got Spanish or Indian blood. Brown skin, brown eyes. Just light make-up, a brush of mascara. Always wearing bandanas or neck scarves. Fancy colours, all different ways. Beads and bangles some days! Have you noticed? The way she struts, pushes her bum out?" It was Sally sounding off. *Maybe not liking the rivalry Cassandra presented*. Marg thought. *Sally was the one used to being the centre of attention in the pub and on the street.*

"My Norm was bowled over when he saw her," Gina went on. Thought it must be a film star, or the Central Queensland Miss Australia candidate visiting Rainworth Downs! Whatever for?"

"More likely a working girl. One of them professional escorts." Sally said.

"Has she been to the salon? Gwen?" Gina inquired.

"No," Gwen Lambert spoke up for the first time. "The first day she was here she popped in to have a look and introduce herself. Said she'd make an appointment some time on her day off."

"Do you think she'll stay here long?" Gina continued. "She's not our type. Too la-de-da if you ask me. Already has that teacher guy in tow. The one with the little Suzuki four-wheel drive."

"Squeak!" Sally blurted out. "That one. His father's the chief Park Ranger in Roma. Looks after Carnarvon National Park. Both too Green for the Comet bar."

After the two other customers had left, Marg was invited into one of the chairs, as Gwen spoke. "That Cassie woman from the bank's living with you, I hear."

"Yes, she's no trouble. A little strange. Won't talk much about her life. Very quiet and polite. She gets on well with Fred. Doesn't much like me asking questions."

"Sally sounded off as usual. Needs something to grumble about. Whinging like a starved crow. Needs to get laid, but the guys are wary. That's the talk."

"It's right, Cassie went out with Andy Thomas to that Ka Mundi area off the Tambo Road. All day Sunday. Came back with some splendid photos. Fred told her she should enter some in the local shows as soon as she gets a chance. He says she's sure to win a prize. She has a brand-new fancy camera."

"I suspect all the town knows by now, about the two of them. Not much escapes notice around here."

"While she was away on Sunday, her sister called. Said her name was Alana Alvarez, then gave a little 'oops' sound like she hadn't meant to say her family name. She wanted to know how Cassie was doing, and was most surprised to hear she had gone out with the male teacher. She said to tell

Cassie that she had a parcel ready to send by courier—a new tennis racquet, tennis dress and shoes, and hiking boots, and some books. I went to ask questions about her name, but she cut me short and hung up."

Fred Bleakley left the bar and moved to sit with Marg when she came in. "I've ordered the barramundi for both of us, if that's okay?"

"Yes," she replied, her mind elsewhere. "The barra's usually very nice."

"I spoke with old Gordon Brassington. He remembers the St. Matthew's Day brawl in 98. It was a Monday. He claims all the trouble was caused by greenies from Brisbane and even inter-state arriving on the Sunday to support the indigenous groups in their protest. It was just our local shire back then before the State Government forced the amalgamation of shires. Les Smallbone, the young Shire Clerk, came out the office to front the protesters, demanding them to leave, and saying a police contingent from Rocky was on its way. He said the crowd were waving '*NO DAMN DAM'* signs and shouting, 'Bring out the Mayor!' over and over as a chant. Mayor Donovan was thought to be the main supporter of the proposed dam and a shareholder in the mining venture that was desperate for a water license."

"Did Gordon remember exactly what happened then?"

"He said the mob got more and more impatient till a few of them rushed forward, knocking Les down as they stormed in the Shire office door. The Mayor and local member had both been escorted out by the police through a back entrance. All the protestors found inside were two scared female clerks, the accountant, the receptionist, and a cleaner."

"So that was the start of Les's back problem." Marg added.

"Yes, Gordon said Les had fallen heavily on his back and fractured his spine. He had surgery and eventually got back on his feet, but never recovered fully."

"He has that unfortunate stoop and no doubt lives with a lot of pain, poor blighter."

The meal came. They thanked the kitchen girl, and Fred gave her his usual gold coin tip.

She smiled back at the friendly bearded face and accepted it. "Thank you, Mister Bleakley."

They talked on as they ate.

"Remember, we were at school and only got the news of the riot at lunchtime. By the time school was out, the town was quiet with a dozen or more police patrolling the street, ready to stop any more trouble."

"You know, I suspect a lot of the farmers and graziers were opposed to the dam proposal but had backed off getting involved."

"Gordon said the reason for that was the Catholic Priest, Father Carrol, had given a fiery St. Matthew's Day eve sermon at mass on the Sunday. The priest quoted Matthew, '*Therefore, do not worry about tomorrow, for tomorrow will worry about itself. Each day has enough trouble of its own.*' And went on, saying to the congregation, '*that arguing and protesting generates bitterness and riot, not peace and harmony. Peace be the way of the Lord*'."

Chapter 5

Tuesday, 29 August 2016

The geography class was full of smirks and whispers, as they filed into Mister Thomas's room on Tuesday morning expectant of some reaction from their teacher to the rumours about his romance.

"Okay. I get it, what's exciting you! But my private life is no business of any of you, right, Guy?" As he pointedly nodded towards the young rebel. "We have work to do, to get on with the project."

"Sir, we might have to get that report on loan from the State Library or buy one through Trove at the National Library." It was Jonathan's strained voice.

"The one on the Comet River environmental study?"

Jonathan nodded. "But, Sir, I've found some other references that are available online," handing a list to his teacher.

It read:

'The Benefits of Water Infrastructure Developments in the Emerald Area, 2008
Comet River Drainage Sub-Basin Wetland Protection Study, 2010

Central Highland Regional Council Flood Mitigation Report, 2011
Comet Sub-Basin Environmental Values and Water Quality Objectives, 2011'

"Thanks, Jonathan, I'll make copies of this list for you all. The documents can be looked up here on your iPads or at home on computers. There is also a study of the Nathan Dam on the Dawson River that never got built, so Jonathan might be able to search for that. Some of the technical information will be very difficult for you but try your best to make some sense of it."

Then, Andy went on to hand out maps of the Comet River Drainage Basin. "I want you to use Google Earth as we did for the Canberra study and see if you can identify any crop farming and coal mines in the area covered by the map. Getting familiar with the map and remote sensing images will help before our field trip next Tuesday. Also the Queensland Government has just released Queensland Globe, a mapping and data online interactive tool, to explore Queensland maps, imagery, and other spatial data. It will give you even more information once you learn how to use it."

That evening, Andrew was reviewing in his mind how his class was coping with the simulation project. Skye and Jonathan were thriving, Jenny, Mandy, and Guy were enthusiastic. Seb, not yet switched on but would light up when he took them into the field and Kongabula Country. Janet and Danielle were country-bred horsewomen. They would be diligent in their own way, following the example of the others. Josie, of course, was struggling, her myopia a serious handicap. Grace always wanted to please, but her commitment to family and family values meant she would be lost in the research demands of the class exercise. He resolved, he would need to provide special help to the latter two.

Thursday, 1 September 2016

In the Thursday class, the teams were all busy searching the information sources and making notes, seeking help from Mister Thomas where needed. When Jonathan announced he'd found information on the proposed Nathan Dam on the Dawson which would be a much bigger storage than any dam if built on the Comet; and there was a speech by a Senator about the urgent need for water infrastructure in Central Queensland to provide water for new large coal mines, agricultural development, and town water supply.

Andrew drew three circles on the whiteboard. A small one representing a Comet River dam, one five times the area representing the relative size of the Nathan Gorge Dam on the Dawson and a bigger one again for the existing Lake Fairbairn on the Nagoa.

"Note the size comparison, we are not talking about a huge water supply yield with our dam."

"So does that mean, Sir, that if the coal mines take over half of it, the farmers, the cattlemen's feedlot operation, and the town won't be greatly better off."

"That is possibly true, Jonathan. Now, you can help the others download where to find useful references. So get on with it! I'm not spoon-feeding you. You will need to understand what is meant by base flow in the river and the difference from flood flows. The dramatic flood flows of December 2010 and March 2011 have been described as a once-in-a-hundred-year event. And there was another smaller flood last year which you will remember."

At the end of the lesson, the field excursion notice was handed out to be taken home with a permission form for their parents to sign.

Jenny Grant was not the only student surprised by the details in the notice. As she walked home, she thought to herself, a habit she had when alone. *It's just a week away. My grandfather, Stanley Sturgess, is to come with us as the local expert on birds. That doesn't seem like keeping the families out of the class project. I know Grandad is a fanatical birdo, but Guy and Seb are sure to think him eccentric and make fun of him. Strange, there's no direct mention of the 'proposed dam study'. Apparently, we are to investigate the wetlands and the irrigation farming in the Comet River basin. The itinerary includes visiting Lake Nuga, Brown Lake named by Leichhardt, and some lagoons and marshlands in addition to the irrigated farmlands downstream. The last stop, seeing the existing Comet Weir near the little settlement of Comet, seems the most relevant to the project. I suppose Sir has his reasons. I wonder what mother will say. Not the cost, but about the inclusion of her father. It seems like a backflip about consulting family, or a sly way of introducing an environmental protection issue.*

Skye went home very excited about the trip. Her thoughts were strictly on topic. *If I understood clearly what I had learnt about sedimentary rock strata since the lesson about stratigraphy, a dam site along the Comet River would be difficult to find. There may be answers provided if we ask the right questions during the excursion.*

Saturday, 3 September 2016

On the Saturday, Cassie rode to tennis on her bicycle. She was excited but unsure how she'd be received in the new tennis dress and tennis shoes and with her new top-grade ladies' racquet in a bag on her back. Andy greeted her with an approving whistle. "Nice dress. You look serious. You've come to play!" But then, he discretely backed off and let the ladies have their say.

On the court, Cassie and Penny played the first match against Skye and Beverley, a cousin of Claudia, she'd been told, and the top female player in the Rainworth Downs Tennis Club. It was a tussle but eventually, she and Penny went down 6–4. Cassie felt she played well, just was mildly unhappy she couldn't win her serve. *It's nerves*, she thought to herself, *the tightness I remember when close to winning a set as a junior and couldn't serve it out. I'd win the match the next game but finish in tears, because that bloody coach expected better.*

"You hit some amazing shots, especially on the backhand," Penny said in praise. "I'm used to losing, playing against Beverley and Skye, but we gave them a fright."

Cassie went on court again when Andy asked her to play with him in a mixed doubles and with confidence rising and Andy's brilliance at the net she won both her serves.

"What don't I know?" Andy asked as they sat together in the clubhouse during the afternoon tea break. "You must have been a good junior to be playing so well after a long break."

"I had a bad fall off a mountain bike," Cassie replied. "Broke my right wrist and tibia badly. Couldn't play for six months. Just gave it away after that."

Andy noticed the little tears forming in the corner of her eyes. How beautiful she looked at that moment of sadness. He took up her right hand from the table and kissed it.

"That's why your forehand and serve are weaker than your backhand, where you have the support of the left arm."

"I know, I'll have to do strengthening exercises. A physio did work on me for nearly a year, but I never got back on the court. Even tried doing a Nadal and playing left-handed."

Andy could tell she was troubled. "I don't believe you're telling me the whole truth."

"I can't tell you here." Then, after a pause, "Can you take me bushwalking again tomorrow? I'd like that. Want to do more nature photography."

"Yes," his face lighting up like he'd won the lottery. "Actually, I was going to ask you if you'd come with me to check out the stopping points on the student field trip. That's on Tuesday. It's for the geography class, part of their project. I suppose you know about that."

"I get the impression everyone in town knows. It has stirred up some old memories, Fred and Marg said. Something to do with a riot back in 1998."

"Yes, unfortunately the old history is getting in the way. Compromising a good class activity. Teaching the students to think like geographers, not just learning facts. Good teaching is about process. Like the way I'm sure you got to know a lot more about your body and the slow progress of healing when you broke your arm. People learn best when they see the need to understand."

Cassie squeezed his hand tightly and smiled back at him as if to say, *'Yes, teacher.'*

"I'm sorry, now I'm boring you."

"No, you can tell me more about your life's mission tomorrow. As long as you promise to return the favour and listen to me. Please? I can be ready at 7 a.m."

"That's great!" Then he left her, pushing forward his tea mug for the washing up. "I see the guys want me for a men's set."

Cassie took both their mugs and went to help Skye with the washing up.

"You haven't told him, have you?" Skye snarled at her. "That you were a State junior champion at 13. You're so secretive."

"I have good reasons for my privacy. Please don't go telling others what you know. I'll tell Andy everything…if and when I'm ready. I need to know him better first. As I said before, know I can trust him."

"I don't want to be cruel, but at the moment, with trouble brewing in the town over this geography project, Mum says, you're a distraction Sir could do without."

Cassie's eyebrows shot up and her mouth gaped open as she dropped the plastic mug she was wiping and threw down the tea towel. "Excuse me, I need to go to the toilet!"

When Cassie had composed herself and returned, Skye was still sitting in the stand, watching Andy in the men's doubles match.

"How about a game of singles with me? There's a spare court. I always preferred singles to doubles."

Skye looked up with a confronting smile. *Yes, and you want to make a fool of me,* she thought to herself.

"You are keen, aren't you? To impress Andy even more! But I'm not good enough. Ask Beverley. She's about to come off from the women's doubles. You'll have a real match against her!"

Sleepless nights, tossing and turning, the persistent effort needed to hold back the tears had become a commonplace part of life for Connie Alvarez, now Cassie Alvos. That was the pattern ever since that damned event at the tennis training camp in 2006. The past week being blessed each night with a full night's sleep had been wonderful, but on the Saturday night after tennis, she couldn't hold back the tears. It wasn't just Skye's words. It was the way she had entered Andy's world, and yet couldn't be open with him about her past—the child abuse, the stalking and street attacks, the ongoing depression, the fear of the royal commission which was promising justice and healing but would, through the exposure, deliver more agony to the victims. She wondered about calling off the outing with Andy, pretending to be sick. But her mother's voice kept telling her, '*No! Giving in means returning to depression and more suicide attempts. You must be strong. Believe in your future.*'

Chapter 6

Sunday, 4 September 2016

Andy blew the Suzuki's horn, as he pulled up at the Bleakley's cottage. Cassie emerged dressed like the previous Sunday but wearing shorts rather than jeans, and boots and gaiters not sneakers. She carried a picnic basket and her camera.

"Good morning, sunshine," Cassie said, trying to be cheery and hopping aboard.

"Glad you could join me. You look tired, sorry it's such an early start."

"It's not that. I just had trouble sleeping, worried about being a 'punishment' you don't need. Making your life more complicated."

"Rubbish!" Andy said, starting the vehicle. "Let's get going. We're off to Lake Nuga Nuga, our first stop."

Out on the Dawson Highway heading south, Andy eased into conversation. "I spoke to my father last night. He's the chief QPWS ranger in Roma, responsible for all the Carnarvon area. I'd like you to meet him. He's a great bloke, my dad. My best mate. He does some part-time tennis coaching. He coached me as a junior. I disappointed him when I dropped out of the tournament circuit. That was when I started Uni in Brisbane. Decided that the tournament scene wasn't for me."

"So like me, you were a good junior and gave it away."

"When I asked Dad could he remember a Cassandra Alvos, a very good junior in the Rocky area, perhaps four or five years younger than me. One that might have suddenly dropped out?"

Andy stole a look at Cassie, trying to discern her reaction, but she went on staring straight ahead, giving nothing away.

"He said he'd definitely have remembered if she had a name like Emmerson—a famous name in Australian tennis, but not a name that had no history. He said there was this one young junior they called 'The Spanish Girl'. She was very boyish. Had her hair cropped really short and wore a cap backwards like Leyton Hewitt. Very aggressive on the court in the way that Gavin Davis, the state junior coach at the time, promoted. He had convinced the girl's mother, a lovely Spanish woman who ran a successful dance school in Rockhampton, that the kid would do best by attending his training camps in school holidays." He paused but Cassie still did not comment.

"When my dad said that, about the mother, it sparked a memory; an image that I've carried with me from that time—a woman who was so striking in appearance and moved so gracefully. A woman who, as a teenager, I felt compelled to look out for in the crowd without really understanding why."

He waited. Didn't prompt her any further but wishing for a response. It was less than a 30-minute drive to get to Nuga Nuga at the north end of the Arcadia Valley, and they were over half way. He wished she would speak. Any comment would do. It was easier to raise sensitive matters when you had an excuse not to look directly at her.

"Let me explain, my history," she offered and the tension fell away from him. "My dad came from Barcelona to Rockhampton with his young bride in 1984. He had been hired to tackle some problems at the Pilbeam Theatre. He's an acoustical engineer—solving problems with sound in live theatres and concert halls. Once they were settled, my mother set up a dance school in Rocky, teaching Spanish and Latin dancing, but then she fell pregnant with Alana and with me three years later. By that time, most of my dad's work was in the major theatres in Brisbane or even Sydney and Melbourne. He was much in demand by theatre architects and production companies, and would only be home for short visits. So mum packed us up and we moved to Brisbane."

"So you're a Brisbane girl, not a Rocky kid."

"Yes for a while, but mum and dad split. She found out he had some other intimate lady friends. She brought Alana and me back to Rocky and re-established her dance school in her maiden name, Alvaresz. It's the family name Alana and I use."

They turned off the highway on the side road to the lake. "Look at that," Cassie exclaimed, seeing all the trees in the lake were dead. "Big eucalypts, all of them. What happened to the trees? Were they poisoned?"

"The lake is a recent phenomenon. A flood coming out of the Carnarvon Ranges deposited a huge load of gravel and clay in the Brown River and created the wall for this shallow dam. The tree roots became waterlogged and so all those big trees have all died."

"It's sad," Cassie said, "rather than beautiful…like me. Like I mostly feel."

Andy was at a loss how to respond, as he pulled the car into the picnic area.

There was a family parked nearby, and the children were throwing bread to the ducks and swans.

Cassie asked if she could include the children in some photographs, and the parents agreed. So she got busy taking care to capture the delight of both the children and the birds, checking the light and focus to fade out the background in some of the shots. When she was satisfied, she showed the children and parents the images on the camera screen, explaining which ones she would keep and which ones she would discard. She took down the father's email address and promised to send them the three or four best shots.

Andy had watched in admiration. "You're an artist, not just a snap-happy photographer. The camera is your brush and palette."

"Just experimenting," she replied, and he loved the broad smile.

A pelican swooped low and landed, skidding over the water to come to rest near the shore. "Damn!" Cassie cried. "Missed it! Wasn't ready in film mode," as she photographed the bird, nevertheless.

"The ducks and coots are always here, but the big birds, pelicans, swans, and magpie geese are visitors, stopping off perhaps while migrating." His comment prompted a question. "Do you feel like that, just dropping in for a short stopover, respite in Comet Country. I don't know that you're here to stay."

"We'll see," she replied, "Maybe, I'll get to love the place."

They walked back to the vehicle. "It's still too early to sample what's in the hamper. Shall we go for a walk? There are sites I would like to show you in the hills. You can't take your camera. It's a secret place. Sacred to the Kongabula people."

"How do you know about it, if it's secret?"

"This is a small National Park, one of several in the Central Highland that my father manages as the Chief Ranger for the district. A man named Jim Gasteen first proposed the park to preserve some of the brigalow country and wanted it called Kongabula."

"And now, it's Nuga Nuga."

"Yes. For political reasons, it was finally called Nuga Nuga when it was gazetted as a National Park—literally perhaps for dead tree, dead tree, the plural form in the indigenous languages. It was my father and Uncle Barry Brownlea, grandfather of one of my students, who showed me around in the protected area."

"All names are convenient tags. I told you that before. What they really mean to the speaker or writer is based on experience. Every time you climb a hill or swim in a river, it gives its name another layer of meaning. It is an engagement between you and the place. This place has pleasant memories for you, I can tell, and every time you say Nuga Nuga they come flooding back into your subconscious. And that bird again, the whistling kite, I can hear it in the distance. It too will have layers of memory."

“Well, Miss Philosopher, follow me!”

“So now I’m a philly, with a ‘ph’.”

Andy laughed as he led her on a winding route through the Brigalow scrubland, around the base of the cone shaped Mount Warrinilla at the northeast end of the lake. When they reached a marked tree at the base of a steep rocky slope, he headed uphill.

“I had to come this way to be sure I could find the workshop.”

“You’re teasing me, Andy. Who’d build a workshop out here in the hills?”

“You’ll see.”

After climbing for ten minutes, they came to a small sandstone cliff where spring water trickled over ferns and moss.

“It’s lovely, this moss garden, but where’s your workshop.”

“Just around here.”

A layer of hard metamorphosed sandstone formed a bench about chest high. On the bench scattered through the dust were small flints of stone. Pieces that had been flaked off larger stones while making cutting tools or spearheads. On the wall above the bench, stencil type ochre paintings depicted stone axes, spears and boomerangs—hunting weapons of the Kongabula.

“The rock here is chert,” Andrew explained. “A secondary deposit within the sandstone layers. Excellent for tool making. And those grooves on the edge of this shelf are where tools were sharpened, or implements were grounded into shape.”

"Streuth! So it truly is a factory," Cassie said in amazement.

"Yes. Possibly has been for thousands of years. Come this way, there's more."

Across another sloping quartzite bench was a set of kangaroo tracks carved into the rock, and then another set, this time more claw like, possibly representing a lace monitor with drag grooves for the tail. More tracks were carved into the wall above, and a rock overhang protected more ochre art—fish shapes and hand stencils.

"It's an art gallery. So well preserved."

"And look at these oval-shaped vulva grooves." He pointed to five of them together and others higher up amongst the rock art.

"Vulva?" Cassie's right hand went up to her face, hiding her mouth, her eyes, hiding her embarrassment.

"Vulva, the most special and magical part of the female body," Andy continued, oblivious to Cassie's distress. "These vulva-shaped carvings occur in rock shelters in Carnarvon Gorge and all throughout the Carnarvon Ranges."

"If that's what they represent, I think it's crude, bordering on porn." The anger welling up inside her.

"They were not carved so as to either excite or poke fun. It's believed they represent fertility. The survival of the tribe." Andy protested.

Almost absentmindedly, he took up a sharp stick to clear an old mud-wasp's nest from one of the smaller vulva carvings.

"Stop it!" Cassie yelled at him. "That's an awful thing to do. She might be a virgin!"

He looked at her, imploring for understanding. “I just—”

But she cut him off, “Don’t make excuses. That’s a criminal act, violating a young woman. You’re disgusting! I had hoped you’d be better than that!” The anger fighting to take control and the tears searching for absolution.

Aghast, he tried to find words to console her, yet his lips remained silent, so he stepped closer, imagining he might comfort her in a hug.

She pushed him away. “You bloody animal! Take me home!” she screamed. “Get me fucking out of here!”

“Where? Bleakley’s? Rockhampton? Spain?”

“Anywhere, you bloody fool! Anywhere but here!” And she set off, scrambling back down the rocky hillside, leaving her hat for Andy to retrieve, leaving him feeling reviled and helpless.

He picked up the hat and rushed to keep up, wishing he’d read the signs. Wishing he hadn’t brought her into Kongabula country—to the secret site. He’d showed her the carvings, acted against Uncle Barry’s, the clan people’s wishes. His indiscretion was destroying him, as it was her.

At the lake shore, Cassie’s screaming sent all the water birds into the sky screeching, the air itself resounding with alarm and anger. Magpie Geese honking, honking, honking. She went straight to the Suzuki, bashing the bonnet and windscreen with her left arm, the stronger one, and then her head. Five, ten times. Not thinking. Not feeling the physical pain.

When he caught up, Andy left her alone till the rage began to subside. Then, he moved to hold her by the shoulders. “Cassie! Calm down, you’re damaging yourself, not my Suzy.”

"It's you who's damaged me, bringing me here!" she screeched. "You don't know how fucking badly. Please take me back to Rainworth."

They drove back in silence, Andy's eyes fixed, unflinching on the road. The speeding didn't concern him. Life was no longer so precious. He had lost faith in the idea of love. Love brought with it a price to pay.

Andrew Thomas returned to his house. He was pleased his two housemates, fellow teachers, were out with friends. He took out the port. He'd only been seriously drunk twice before and afterwards had hated how he'd poisoned his body, how he took more than a full 24 hours to recover. Still, it was only half a bottle so he went for it, seeking release.

In the evening, Penny Mattingley phoned.

"What happened?" she asked. "I was there with Marg, when you arrived back before lunch. I was waiting for Skye and her classmates who were with Fred over at 'The Blockhouse', doing research on your class project. What upset Cassie so much? She rushed to her bedroom, mouthing some obscenities. Ignoring us!"

"I cun't…talk 'bout it," he answered in a slurred voice. "S'all my stu—pid ffoult."

"Marg phoned Cassie's sister, asking to speak to the mother. She wasn't there. The daughter didn't know when to expect her, but promised to get the mother to call back."

"Mother's name's, Alver—ez. Leas that's na—im she uses. Has a dance schoool…in Rocky. Tells me…driving out to Nuga…"

"So that's where you were. The only words Marg got out of Cassie was something about an aboriginal gallery that disgusted her. I think those were the words. We thought you might have gone all the way into Carnarvon Gorge to see the art galleries."

"There's a spec…il site…north side of mount…Warrin…illa. Not faar from lake. Kept secret. Schouldn't hav been there. Now thing's gone arse up! I'm a bloooddy fool. Cassie told me off in a terrible rage. Stampeeded all the birds."

"I'm sorry to hear that. Don't blame yourself. I suspect she's fired up by something from her past. Some awful memory. Perhaps, Marg will find out more when she speaks to Misses. Alveresz."

"Thanks Penny. Thank's fa ya concern. I need ta sleep on it. Douse this whole tragic day outa my head."

Chapter 7

Monday, 5 September 2016

"Morning, Sir. Thanks for the sandwiches and fruit yesterday," Guy and Skye said together as Andy Thomas arrived and approached his staff room. "We want to tell you what we found out at 'The Gregory Blockhouse' yesterday."

He was brusque with them. "Not here, come to my classroom in ten minutes."

The two students were already seated when Andy Thomas arrived at the room. "Well, what's so exciting? I can't give you much time. Mister James wants to see me before first lesson."

"That book. The one about the environmental impact of the proposed Comet River Dam at the Starlee site," Guy spoke up. "It was there in the small library. All three volumes of it."

"Yes, and Mister Bleakley let me take volume one home. It has the full summary of the report, maps, and statistics as well," Skye went on. "It's a goldmine of relevant information for our project. It doesn't take sides. Just brings together all the facts."

"I'm glad you found it. But don't keep it just to your group. You must share the information around the class."

"We also found out about the protest over the previous dam proposal led by the local indigenous elders and out of town Greenies from a number of conservation groups—how it got out of hand and Mister Smallbone was injured. Mister Bleakley told us the story."

"It was St. Matthew's Day, 21 September 1998." Skye added.

"Well, really that is not relevant to our study. That's old history. Not part of our geography study. But the environmental impact information is very important. Now, I have to go. See you in class tomorrow."

The school secretary greeted Andy at the office. "He's on the phone, just take a seat Mister Thomas, I'm sure he won't be long."

Andy waited impatiently as the call dragged on for five more minutes. He could tell the conversation was heated. *Possibly an angry parent about a lost lunch box or the amount of homework—either too much or not enough.*

"Andy, come in close the door."

"Some problem?"

"Yes, that was the regional director on the phone from Emerald. You won't like this, but she has ordered me to call your field excursion off."

"But it's tomorrow! We have the parent's permission all except little Josie's, but I'm expecting that today. And all the money's paid. I'll pay for Josie if she doesn't have the money with her today. Her parents are prospecting at Anakie and her grandma may be desperate for cash."

"There are too many complaints. Les Smallbone from the regional council, the local Glenline mine boss and the chief executive at the Pungara South project have joined forces and lobbied to have you transferred out of the Central Highlands region as soon as possible."

"Why? What have I done that is so wrong? The class project is not about their bloody mines. This is wrecking a great teaching project! The students will be annoyed. Explosive! They have put so much effort in already. Bugger! Excuse me but this is a cruel decision! I don't know how I can break it to them!"

"They raised some petty things, like a male teacher taking out a class of nearly all girls, and no female teacher with them; and the danger of snakes in the paddocks, and cattle being stirred up and stampeding through fences."

"Well, that's all ridiculous. And if you can't spare a female teacher or teacher's aide, there's always Marg Bleakley, I believe she still has her teaching registration and would surely help out."

"But the other objections are more serious, like stirring up old sores with some farmers who don't want to give up water allocations to the coal mines, and rumours circulating that the town will get flooded and have to be moved. That was the threat with the project proposal in the 1990s."

"But that is stupid again, because the project the class is discussing is theoretical, and those community toffs and the town's people surely know it. It is not as if this is for real. It's a simulation exercise. And the fake proposal is for a dam well upstream from Rainworth Downs. The only feasible site up river is just below Lake Nuga Nuga, which the students would find out on the excursion. If there was such a dam built, it would flood part of Nuga Nuga National Park, and I couldn't see any Queensland Government having the courage to do that!"

"Okay, you've said your piece, but it is now out of my hands."

"Well, it shouldn't be my responsibility to tell the class! I had a rotten day yesterday and right now, today is turning out worse. I feel absolutely gutted."

"Yes, I understand that I have to do that. I'll call all the Year 10s to come to the hall at morning recess, and announce it then. Also explaining that the trip money will be refunded. Andy, there's no joy in this for me either."

Cassie woke when Marg Bleakley knocked on the door to offer her coffee. It was already 10 a.m. She could see Marg was concerned about her, but she didn't want to talk. "No thanks, not now. Maybe later."

"I'll bring it anyway and a piece of toast. You need to drink and eat a little."

She remembered crying all afternoon and into the early hours of the morning, mulling over the sickening agony that had flooded over her on a day which had promised so much. Her mind was still in turmoil. She hadn't undressed from the outing, only taken off the boots and gaiters.

It was Fred who brought the coffee. "Here, my lady, you need a bit of sustenance. Marg has phoned Smithson at the bank and explained you won't be in for a couple of days. Don't brood too much. Try to look on the bright side. Andy's a great bloke. Whatever happened, I'm sure he meant you no harm. I suspect he's hurting too. Penny Mattingley told us how well you two were getting on."

"Thanks, Fred, I need some more private time."

To pass the time while the emotional ache subsided Cassie switched on her computer and loaded her new photos. She was glad there were none from the aboriginal factory site, just the lovely ones of the lake and the children feeding the water birds. Then, she flicked back to the previous photo set and stopped at the one with Andy and his reflection in the pool at the spring. *What do I see in him? The reflection, I want to admire and love; or a man, crude and base, like so many others? Was he grooming me, so flattering and attentive, a ruse intended to seduce and take advantage. Intercourse without consent? Rape? Yet in my heart I want to believe he's sincere.*

She went back further to the images of the dancing brolgas in the field. She thought of a quote she had found on the net with its warning to young lovers, *wrong turns, and despair often litter the road of romance. You can't escape being hurt if you're going to open yourself up to love.* What was the attraction of this man who had come into her life, as if sent to rescue her from herself. He didn't fit her image of country town men. He wasn't a cowboy, all false style and bluster. No Stetson leather hat with turned up rim, no glamorous belt with a large brass buckle, no crumpled well-worn jeans. He was sensitive, chivalrous, percipient. She had treated him abominably, failed to explain her grief. Her fear, her distrust of her own vulva. She should have cushioned him, cautioned him about getting too involved. Explained her medication, what it was for, the likely side-effects. Been honest with him. Now, it was too late.

Seb Goodman was checking the tyre pressure on a car in the driveway of his dad's garage when Andy pulled into a parking spot.

"Hi, Seb, why weren't you at school"

"Dad had a big job on, two mine trucks, and he needed an extra hand."

"Hello, Andy, come to check up on Seb truanting again?" Seb's father approached out of the workshop smiling as usual and wiping grease off his hands with an old towel. When he first came to Rainworth Downs, Andy had engine problems with the Suzuki and he'd soon found that Sam Goodman was a good mechanic and conducted an efficient business.

"Sorry, I really needed Seb today. He's already good with tuning engines, and I also wanted help with some of the heavy work, the truck tires that needed to be taken off to get to the brake cylinders."

"Why look who's here," It was Angie, Seb's mother, the daughter of Uncle Barry Brownlea. As with other times, he was at the garage, Andy couldn't help thinking, *She's a beautiful woman in her early 30s and mother of five. She reminds me of Deborah Mailman, not just the looks, but the voice as well. That film star quality.*

"Just dropped by to let Seb know the field trip for tomorrow has been called off. The Regional Director of Education told my boss that it had to be cancelled."

"We heard Les Smallbone sounding off about it," Sam offered, "when he was here the other day. I suppose he pulled some strings and got it stopped. What a bugger for you and the kids. It's a real pity."

Then, Angie added with a clarity Andy admired. "Seb was looking forward to it. He doesn't much like school 'cept for seeing his footy mates, but it's surprised us how he loves your geography classes and the activities you have the students doing. He didn't select metal work, like most of the Year 10 boys, because he felt he couldn't learn anything that he hadn't already learnt from his dad. That true, Seb?"

The boy nodded, "I like geography. It's about country. Can we keep going and finish the project anyway?"

"We'll have to see. Be in class tomorrow and we'll discuss it."

Then, Angie beckoned Andy into the service station shop. "You might like to know there were two women called in a half hour ago for fuel and directions to 'The Gregory Blockhouse'. Said they'd just driven out from Rockhampton. New model Mazda sedan. The younger one looked so like the new woman, Cassie, isn't it, at the National Bank—the word is, Streuth, that you are already courting her. Didn't get a good look at the other one, but I suspect she is the mother," she went on in a whisper as another customer entered. "I don't know if that's good news or bad news."

"Cassie and I had a big bust up yesterday. That relationship might be all over as quickly as it started. I must go. Make sure Seb is at school tomorrow."

Andy was not surprised when his phone rang while he and his housemates were having dinner. It could be a parent or even one of his students, but it was Fred Bleakley.

"Excuse me, Fred. We are part way through dinner. I'll take this in my room."

In his bedroom, he answered. "What is it Fred?"

"Cassandra's mother and sister are here in town."

"Yes, I guessed that. Angie Goodman told me about the two women asking directions to 'The Blockhouse'. She'd noticed the younger one looked like Cassie, same colouring, slim body, and dress sense. Didn't get a good look at the older one who stayed in the car."

"While the sister, Alana, was in the bedroom with Cassandra, trying to console her, Marg and I had a good chat with the mother. There's a lot you don't know."

"I gathered that. I was stupid showing Cassie the aboriginal carvings in the hills behind Mt. Warrinilla, not far from Lake Nuga Nuga. We were having a lovely time till then. Till she exploded. Told me I was a child molester. Shouting at me. You should have heard all the screeching, Cassie and the water birds, those magpie geese honking."

"Marg told Misses. Alverez about Cassie enjoying the tennis club and about the bush walk you two did in the Carnarvon National Park. We talked about the photos Cassie took, how good they were. That's when Alana called her mother into the bedroom. We weren't a party to what transpired."

"Thank Marg for me. Both of you. You've been great."

"Before they left, they said they would like to meet with you, and Penny Mattingley also. They are staying at the Comet Motel but left Cassandra with us. Said they hoped they could get her to go back to work by Wednesday."

"Thanks, Fred, for the call. I was expecting some of my geography class's parents to phone. The field trip we were doing tomorrow has been cancelled by order of the Regional Director of Education."

"That's Lyn Sutcliffe in Emerald. Pretty bossy type. Quick on the draw, you might say. And Doug James is a junior principal. He'd have to cave in to save his own position."

"Well, I haven't had the pleasure of meeting Ms. Sutcliffe. Can't say I want to."

"Keep your chin up Andy. Things like this blow over. In a year's time, you'll be wondering what all the fuss was about."

Streuth, he thought as he walked back to the dining room to finish his meal. *It has many connotations, that word.*

Having finished his meal, Andy phoned his father in Roma to tell him not to come to Nuga Nuga to speak to his class as the field trip is off. Gary Thomas listened and then offered some advice.

"Les Smallbone, if he is behind it, is not your enemy, but his own enemy. He has reason to be angry at the world, not just his accident back in '98 but the recent death of Mary, Misses. Smallbone, and his own prostate cancer. Look at the cancellation as an opportunity. Talk with your students. I'd think they would want to finish the project after already working on it for several weeks."

Before Andy could reply, his father went on, "I'll get help in the office and do a YouTube video. I'll be briefly covering the history of the Arcadia Valley settlement scheme, with the loss of the large areas Brigalow vegetation, and the declaration of the Nuga Nuga National Park to protect an important remnant of scrub as well as the lake. I'll include a bit about Jim Gasteen, who was the rural journalist, who first proposed the park using the aboriginal name, Kongabula."

"Well, thanks, that's good of you."

"I'll do it tomorrow and send it on to you. By the way, can you join me on a hike up to Mt. Serecold on Sunday. Want to check out some vandalism in a part of the Serecold State Forest. I'll go in from the south via Rewan Station and meet you at the junction with the State Forest road on your left coming up Consuelo Creek valley. It would be about 50 kilometres for you from Rainworth Downs."

Andy realised he shouldn't disappoint his father, and Cassie in her current mood would not be likely to accept an invitation to go walking with him.

"Yes, I could be there for 8 a.m. if I leave here at 7."

"Good, now I have to go. Your mother and I are running late for night tennis. Hope you are getting on well with 'The Spanish Girl'! Tell me another time."

Chapter 8

Tuesday, 6 September 2016

"We've formed a war council," Guy announced as Andy walked into the classroom for the Tuesday geography lesson. Most lessons, he organised the ten students into workshopping on inquiry activities, using textbooks, maps, photographs, library resources, their tablets, and computers. But it seemed that he was confronted with a delegation that wanted a voice. A protest was not unexpected. Andy had already been informed that parents of seven of the ten students had phoned, complaining about the field trip cancellation, echoing their children's anger about the decision, so he knew there were supporting sentiments amongst the families.

"Okay, what's your proposal?"

"First a virtual field trip," Skye was leading. "You, Sir, present a lesson as if we are on the trip. Maps, photographs, even interviews if you can get it together for our class on Thursday. We can ask questions for each location, the places we would have visited today."

"Blimey. You lot don't expect much, but I'll see what I can do."

Secondly, it was Jonathan, "We have already tapped into quite a lot of resources and the Environmental Impact Study on the 1990s dam proposal has great data that is relevant."

"You must understand that project involved a dam site downstream from Comet Downs at Starlee, not the same as our imagined project. You have to be careful how you use that information."

Then, Jenny Grant took over, "We've had a discussion, and we don't want to continue with the division into for and against teams. We want to work as one group and divide up the tasks amongst us to put together one presentation."

All ten pairs of eyes were fixed on him. Demanding his support.

"Well, I can see some advantages in that if you all pull your weight. Time is limited. The term ends at the end of next week. You need to be realistic, and one of you has to coordinate, write the introduction and the conclusions."

"We're not talking a written report," Skye went on. "We want to put together a first-class power point presentation."

"And," Guy got to his feet. "We'll do it in the hall with the big screen and the new digital projector. We want an audience, not just us and the other year tens." He looked around for confirmation.

We want to present to the parents, reps from the town, and also those who opposed the study and the field trip."

They all clapped. Excited by the passion. The enthusiasm to make it work.

"You do want to put on a show. Don't you. Film it as well I expect."

“Yes!” There was a chorus, and the loudest shout was from Seb, “Show those conservative bastards!”

“Careful, Seb, that language is totally unacceptable.”

“It’s how we feel,” he mumbled and then remained silent, hanging his head.

“Okay, back to your desks. You can divide the presentation into, perhaps, eight segments, each one with a maximum of five Power Point slides. An introductory segment, most likely dam site, physical and economic costs, environmental affects upstream…they called out their suggestions which Andrew wrote on the whiteboard, consolidating some and re-ordering the list till they were satisfied.

“I guess Jonathan, helped by Seb, can handle the technical side, so that leaves eight of you as could-be presenters. You need to agree who plans each group of slides, and who will speak. Don’t leave it all to Skye and Jenny. I’ll talk to Mister James and see if we can do it last day of term.”

Mandy Macpherson put up her hand. “Sir, do you think…?’ Looking around a little scared, they would object to what she had to say.

“Yes, Mandy, you have a better idea?”

“Sir, the presentation. I know it’s the first day of the holidays, and some families might be heading away, but is it possible to do the presentation in the hall on the Saturday night? It would give us the whole Saturday to plan and rehearse to make sure we can do it as well as possible.”

Except for little Josie, Mandy was the smallest and quietest of the class, but Andy knew there was a spirited streak that regularly surfaced. Her father was the local vet and relatively new to the town.

"Well, that has a lot of merit, Mandy, and I'll make the suggestion to Mister James, but all of you and your families would have to go along with it."

Back at the staff room there was a message on his mobile.

'Meet tennis club 4 p.m. C's mum & sister for coffee. Penny.'

Andy packed maps and teaching notes and headed off quickly with his school Toshiba desktop and phone.

Penny Mattingley met him at the clubhouse. "Glad you made it. They wanted to meet over coffee. The town cafe's too busy after school. Not much seating either, so I suggested here. I expect they'll be here soon. How are you? Recovering?"

"It's a bloody shame about the field trip, but the geography class has done a lot to restore my spirits."

"Yes, Skye said they intended demonstrating. I warned her about overdoing it!"

"They stood me up with their grand plans. Guy Lambert led the charge. They want to put on a presentation, report to the whole community. It astounded me. Then, Mandy Macpherson proposed that they do it on Saturday night, first day of the holidays. What you think?"

"I'd say it's a brilliant idea. If they have the courage and add some other entertainment perhaps… Look, here they are, the Spanish deputation."

The Mazda had pulled up, and the two women entered through the clubhouse gate.

He had to think it, *Streuth,* —the resemblance, the hair, the bronze complexion, the elegant style. The images of the mother from his tennis youth flicking back into his consciousness. "Pleased to meet you, Misses. Alverez and Alana," Penny offered, "Meet Andrew Thomas."

Andy said his hellos and ushered them to a table while Penny went to make the coffee.

"I'm so sorry, Misses. Alverez about Cassandra, I didn't mean to—"

She interrupted, "Please call me Lorae. It's not your fault. Alana and I will explain."

Penny returned with cake and biscuits and then the coffee.

"Thank you for the kindness you've shown to Cassandra. You must have already guessed that Cassandra Alvos is an assumed name. Part of the strategy for her to stay out of any limelight, living for a while in a small country town. Her legal name is Consuela Alverez. The girls have taken on my family name. Their father is in Brisbane."

"Cassie told me that much!"

"You might have also gleaned that Connie, Consuela, was a top junior tennis player," Alana said. "I took up the sport first, but Connie was soon much better than me. She won the Queensland Primary School Championship and the State under 14, then gave it up."

"She told us that she had a bike accident, smashed her right arm and wrist," Penny put in.

"True," Lorae went on. "And that's why we all thought she didn't want to go back on the court. Even with the best efforts of the physiotherapists, she couldn't get the strength back in her right arm. Said she never wanted to play again unless she could return to her best."

"And was there another reason?" Penny asked.

"Well. We think Connie should tell you about that herself. Especially you, Andrew. I've talked with her therapist, and we have decided that's the best approach now. She needs you, an Aussie male friend, she can bond with."

"After what happened at Lake Nuga Nuga, I'm sorry, but I want Cassie, Connie, whoever she is, out of my life. I can't live with the hysterics. I can't befriend a drama queen. It's beyond me."

He wiped his teary eyes, but could not hide his stress.

"Marg and Fred Bleakley have told us all about you, even about your geography class project that has stirred up the town." Alana said.

"She needs your help," Lorae pleaded, leaning forward and wiping Andy's eyes with a tissue from her handbag. "I'm a mother fighting for my daughter's life. Hoping for a saviour. A man like you, Andrew, who can give to her what you give to your teaching. The same compassion, same dedication. I can understand you think that it's unfair of me to ask. But I won't give up hope."

Then, she pushed forward a press cutting from the Rockhampton Morning Bulletin dated 14 January 2016.

Woman Dragged from the River

A young woman was dragged from the Fitzroy just after 5 p.m. yesterday evening. She had lead weights strapped around her body and attached to her feet. A North Rockhampton resident who helped in the rescue of the woman applied CPR resuscitation until the ambulance arrived. It is believed the 22-year-old woman, who is now recovering in Rockhampton Hospital, is the daughter of Lorae Alvarez. Ms. Alverez operates the Spanish Dance School in Alma Street. The police reported there was no evidence of foul play.'

Andy read the article, then struggled to read it again. It winded him, his gut sickening and churning.

"My God! Holy hell!" he yelled, then tried to swallow the words into the quagmire inside him. He stood, stamping his feet, mouthing a profusion of other obscenities, desperately endeavouring to drive away the anguish.

He was offering the disquieting newspaper cutting to Penny, when there was a sudden interruption.

"Hello, Mum, Mister Thomas," It was Skye, bubbly as ever. "I went home and you weren't there. I guessed I'd find you here. Came on my bike. Will you introduce me to the visitors?"

The introductions abruptly over Penny Mattingley took her daughter aside. "That was rude of you, Skye, to interrupt us. You should be at home or at netball training, not here!"

"The training was called off, and I was wanting to tell you about our war council and what has been decided for the geography project."

"You could have waited. Cassie's mother and sister wanted a private meeting."

With great effort, Andy gathered his composure and went back to sit opposite Lorae Alvarez. After a while of silent communication he asked quietly, "Please explain."

Lorae took his hand and began the story.

Alana and Penny left them to it and carried the coffee mugs back to the small club house kitchen. "Skye, I believe you're in Mister Thomas's class. I hear he's a very good teacher."

"He's the best. We all love him, the geography class. What's up with Cassie? Is it serious? Is that's why you're here? I hope she's okay."

"We think she'll be fine. A number of things have upset her. Got under her skin. Just needs some understanding friends. Your mother might tell you about it later. The tennis club should be good for my sister. Great to hear she has been back on the court with you guys."

"She's a fantastic player. I wish I was that good."

"Well, Skye, please keep encouraging her. She had previously turned her back on tennis, a sport she was once crazy about. Consuela is an adventurous woman, when you get to know her. Loves the outdoors, being active. She'll treasure Andrew's company if he continues to offer it."

Skye turned away to hide a smirk, a protest. Holy hell! How she too she wanted a response from Andrew—not just in her secret life.

That night, Andy Thomas worked hard to prepare for the virtual field trip. It helped him to take his mind off the Cassie Alvos—the Connie Alverez calamity. His focus must be on his teaching. He needed the students to imagine they were there in the field. Make it real for them. The map of the Comet River catchment and the proposed stopping points was easy, he'd already prepared that. He had filmed a hurried interview with Gareth Mattingley, comparing the Starlee site with its proposed 1.2-kilometre-long wall, and the most suitable site upstream of the town at Warrinilla.

And he could project enlargements around both sites and show the area of the storages in each case up to the proposed full supply level.

His father had come good with the YouTube video. Gary Thomas covered the history of the Arcadia Valley settlement scheme, explaining the loss of the large areas of the Brigalow Belt vegetation, and the declaration of the Nuga Nuga National Park to protect an important remnant of scrub as well as the lake. Jenny Grant's grandfather had provided splendid photographs of birdlife at Lake Nuga Nuga, Lake Brown, and in the other wetlands of significance downstream. The bird watching enthusiast had explained how the whistling kites had taken up nesting in the old dead trees in the lake, and that spectacular flocks of magpie geese were now regular visitors to the wetlands. Andrew hadn't previously known that the geese, once widespread in Australia, were now confined mainly to the far north because of loss habitat and shooting by game hunters. Their presence alone made the lake environmentally significant.

Councillor Simon Stevens, Guy Lambert's uncle, would not speak about any dam but offered an ABC Landline segment filmed at his property. It explained the channelling of water into constructed tanks and the natural billabongs on the flood plains had been a great success since the Starlee project was rejected. The Stevens operation involved broad acre cultivation of sunflower and sorghum crops. Some neighbours grew cotton, but the insecticide sprays used to control aphids and mites had serious management and environmental problems. Too much irrigation could also result in salt problems, and farm chemicals leached into the water table, thus, affecting the quality of water drawn from the many bores throughout the valley.

He could inject statistics about current water usage by irrigators, coalmines, and for domestic use, water from the stream, the Comet Weir downstream, and from bores. There was much publicity in the media about proposed coalmine expansion, so he felt he did not need to elaborate. Perhaps, point out the location of the existing mines on the map and show a couple of photos of open-cut operations.

What he still needed was the words of Uncle Barry Brownlea. Perhaps, he could record a chat with the Kongabula elder. Get him speaking about the burial and carving sites protected in the National Park, and the many stone artefacts from the area that are stored in the museum at 'The Gregory Blockhouse'. He knew what Uncle Barry would say, and he was right. "My people, we big fight 'im dam. Protest before. Fight 'im again! You tell Smallbone mob that! No matter what happened, back that time!"

Thursday, 8 September 2016

Andrew Thomas believed in the flipped classroom pedagogy. He had his students reading source materials or watching videos and documentaries at home, with the class time used to do the harder work of assimilating that information through strategies, such as problem-solving, discussions, and summarising.

"That was great, Sir," both Skye and Jenny commented when he finished, taking the class on the simulated journey in the field. "It will help us select the relevant data for our class power point presentations."

“It’s recorded on Swivl, so I’ll post as a link on the school web page, and you can look at it again at home. Your class time will be precious next week because that’s all the time you’ve got. Not a slack last week of term for you guys.”

“So can we do the Saturday night presentation as Mandy suggested?” Guy asked. “We are all waiting for the answer.”

“Yes! Mister James has agreed as long as none of your parents strenuously object.” There was a spontaneous cheer and clapping.

“What about the education department, and the other dudes who pushed to have our field trip called off,” Guy went on.

“Mister James said they’d be invited, but it wouldn’t be called off whatever they said. It is a community event for Rainworth Downs presented by Year 10 students.”

“My mum said she would get other mums to help her put on some supper,” Seb said enthusiastically.

“I’ve already checked out the technology,” Jonathan revealed. “We can play background music and display a welcome on the screen as people arrive.”

“And we can display maps, photographs, and charts around the walls,” Jenny suggested. “Also project a map onto a white board, the way you have shown us, that can operate as a touch screen.”

“We’re also talking with the music students, not just Year 10s,” Skye added her clinching words, “to put on a couple of items to entice more than just our own families to come along.”

“Well, fantastic, looks like it’s all go!” Andy’s grin stretched across his face, as the class took to their feet in their joy, shaking hands and hugging each other.

Unlike his housemates, Andrew Thomas didn’t take to the indoor gym setup in their spare room. Instead, that evening, he went for a long run around the town past several of the students’ homes, stopping only to do some chin-ups on the high horizontal bar in the exercise area of Gregory Park. When he returned, he showered and got into bed, his thoughts were still spinning. He couldn’t sleep. The previous two nights he had the virtual field trip to focus his brain activity away from the terrible torment he had been closing out of his mind. *Vulva carvings. Screeching. Screeching. Honking Geese. Nuga Nuga. Depression. Suicide. Therapy. Cassandra. Consuela. Suicide. Depression. Honking Geese... Damn! Fucking damn!*

It was torment—an illuminated kaleidoscope of stinging vapidities trashing his desires and doubts into jumbled shards of more and more misery. The pride he had in the response and initiatives of his Year 10 students could not wipe out those tormenting images. To calm himself, he went to the kitchen for a glass of port. There, sitting alone in his pajamas, he recalled Lorae’s explanation, the need for secrecy:

“When at 14, Consuela became so very depressed and would not reveal what was troubling her, I decided to take her on a holiday to Barcelona where my brother has a medical and psychiatric practice. She settled in well in Spain and was much happier under the guidance of her Uncle Climent. She decided to stay away from whatever it was that was destroying her in Australia and finish her schooling in Spain, while I returned home to Australia where I have my dance school. Her uncle encouraged her to take up a new outdoor interest as part of her therapy for depression. Challenged by her male cousins, she tried surfing and soon lost any fear to become proficient riding the big waves. Consuela and the boys travelled to all the top surf beaches in Spain and Portugal, seeking the best surf breaks. She was in love with the sport till, just before she had planned to return to Australia, she was wiped out in a big surf at Mundarka on the Basque coast. She was hit on the head by her own surfboard suffering concussion.

So when she returned home to Rockhampton, she was content with the smaller waves at Yeppoon. She studied accountancy, found work at the National Bank, and settled down to her Australian life, living with myself and Alana. The suicide attempt came out of the blue. Something had reignited her mental health problems and made her desperate. Climent made a rush visit to see what he could do to help her. During the therapy counselling, she revealed to him some details of a sexual assault when she was 13. We knew nothing about it. It was a shock to us. Not easy to deal with. It has become the subject on an ongoing investigation. We chose Rainworth Downs as somewhere she might have the chance of a normal life under an assumed name while the investigation continues. The senior staff at the National Bank cooperated to relocate her to your town."

He returned to the whirlpool in his mind. *Now it's my life, too, that's messed with. Why can't I get this woman out of my mind? I thought I was falling in love with the gorgeous Cassandra Alvos. Now, I'm in despair. How do I face up to being in the presence of 'The Spanish Girl', the Miss Consuela Alverez I know so little about! Is there a way out of her sickness? Is there a way out for me?*

On the same night Connie Alvarez was wondering how she could stay on in Rainworth Downs. It was irrational, she knew, but she wanted this Andrew Thomas in her life—wanted to feel his gentle touch, a soft kiss, a sigh of acceptance that blended into words of affection. Yet she had known him less than a month, and he had other priorities in his life. His teaching was his centre of being. Still, the thought of inviting him to take her into his arms, even possibly…into her bed, would not go away. She kept asking herself, "Was it love or insanity, this passion?"

There was a knock on the door at the Bleakleys. It was Angie Goodman. Fred welcomed her. "Come in," Marg called from the kitchen. "We're both pleased you were able to leave the family behind and visit Cassandra. Maybe, you can be of some help to her."

"I hear she has not been well. Something happened on their outing on Sunday."

"True. She came home so frightfully stressed, later Fred discerned that it has something to do with Aboriginal culture and art, but she won't say more."

"Her mother and sister have come from Rocky to help console her, and she has calmed down quite a lot." Fred added. "They're staying a couple of days in town."

Marg interjected. "I think I should take you to Cassie's room and leave you to chat about aboriginal perspectives on life. We both think it could be very helpful for her, and you are the best one in town by far to do it sensitively."

Angie sat next to the bed beside Cassie. "We Murri people see the world very differently from Europeans. In a hunter-gatherer society, people live day by day. The only calendar is the seasons as experienced and named in relation to the local tribal environment. Life for us First Peoples is really only the present and the Dreamtime—your Anglo word for our spiritual culture. There were no recorded stories in written language. Intellectual knowledge was passed on in folklore—dance, music, song, rock art, and carvings."

"So do you believe those paintings and carvings, Andrew showed me in the hills near Lake Nuga Nuga, are special. Are they some kind of comment on life."

"If it is the well-protected site my father took to me once in the Kongabula country, I know it has stencil art, some more animal paintings in vivid ochre colour, carvings of animal tracks and oval symbols."

"It is the oval carvings that upset me. When Andy called them the vulva carvings, I was horrified. I freaked out."

"The importance of them is that they signify birth and survival. For the Bidgera and Kongabula tribes of the Carnarvon Ranges the female womb and vulva was the source of human life. The environment here can be very harsh—long droughts, violent storms, and flash floods. Tribal groups need to move around their country as local conditions, and the availability of food varies. Population growth is small, if at all. Children die in childbirth, through malnutrition, natural diseases, spider and snake bites, and so on. Living to maturity and middle age is a challenge."

"So Andrew tried to tell me…I wouldn't listen…the vulva carvings are in no way rude or pornographic."

“Certainly not! As I say, they signify tribal milestones, years, maybe thousands of years of having their own territory.”

“Thanks, Angie, that is truly helpful. Helps puts me at peace with myself.”

Angie swept her arms across her body. “This Kongabula woman has had to adjust and learn in the IT age. Now, you are on the reverse journey. I suggest enter a few notes on your phone or laptop. Reflect later and write about your journey as you go.”

“Thanks again,”

Angie stood. Realising she also had soothing tears running over her cheeks.

“Just one more thing,” Angie said, taking out tissues for herself and handing more to Cassandra. “That site, and others in the Kongabula Hills are regarded by my father as sacred. The ancestral spirits don’t want non-indigenous people there. This may seem incredulous to you but not to me…I believe the spirits orchestrated, in their mysterious way, to drive you away by infiltrating your mind and so spooking you to flee. Whatever actually happened on site that stirred up your stress and horror was as much their doing as your own vulnerability. Andrew was very wrong to take you there. Indeed, his own links to being Murrie are somewhat thin. Only his great-grandmother was a Garingbal woman.”

“I will go and join Marge and Fred for a while. Take a few minutes to compose yourself, then please come out to the kitchen and join us.”

Chapter 9

Saturday, 10 September 2016

The twitteras and twitterettes in Rainworth Downs had been busy. On the Saturday morning, they had their tasks to do. Guy and Seb cycled the town, posting flyers about the presentation night in every house mailbox. Skye and Jenny walked the main street, stopping and handing out flyers to residents who arrived to shop. Grace did the same inside her parents' post office shop and news agency. Jane and Danielle rode through the town on their horses, dismounting to attach the A3 posters prepared by the art students onto the notice board at the front entrance to shops and business. The illustrated poster read:

'HEAR YE! HEAR YE!
Imagine a New Dam on the Upper Comet River?
Year 10 students present their analysis of the pros and cons!
Rainworth Downs School Hall, Saturday 17 September at 7:30 p.m.
Displays & Power Point big screen presentation.
FREE musical entertainment & supper provided.'

Then, all the year 10 students gathered for a BBQ at Gregory Park arranged by the Macphersons and sponsored by Comet Hair and the Comet Service Station. Uncle Barry Brownlea, the indigenous elder, and old Stanley Sturgess, the town's bird expert, were welcomed as guests. It was a chance for the students to tap into the knowledge of two senior citizens—each from very different backgrounds, sharing a love of the river.

Andrew Thomas was on the court, playing in a set when the Bleakleys arrived at the tennis centre with Cassandra. For Andy, tennis was habitual. Like driving a car, he could be in automatic gear and enjoy it whatever the score. The exercise was a blessing, taking his mind off the love match, the Avarez affair, where he had no idea of what shots to play.

Cassie went straight to the stand to watch Andy play. She admired his easy style and grace on the court. She clapped his winners, and gave an audible 'ooh' when he made an unforced error. Surely, he noticed her there, yet when he left the court, he nodded to the Bleakleys and headed straight for the toilet. Fred Bleakley went to bring him back, but Penny Mattingley was quick to call out, "No, Fred, let him be. He needs time."

Then, Penny turned her attention to Cassie. The young woman was dressed as if she was out on a casual summer evening date. Hair platted down her back, light lipstick, sunglasses. A floral sleeveless top and navy skirt. Expensive looking heeled sandals. "I see you haven't come to play."

"No. Not in the mood for tennis, despite the lovely weather. I just came, hoping to speak to Andy. I tried his phone but he mumbled something about being busy and hung up."

"He has been busy, steering the Year 10 geography project. He said to me that he didn't know what to say to you. Something about the incident at Nuga Nuga being a lightning bolt to his heart."

"One is slow to recover from a heart attack," Marg put in, "but it need not be terminal. He'll come round."

"Well come and sit at a table and have a cuppa, till he comes out." Penny suggested. "We have some lovely homemade carrot cake and pikelets with plum jam and cream."

"Sounds great," Fred said as he sat next to Cassie and put a hand on her arm in encouragement.

When Andy returned from the locker room, he had showered and changed out of his tennis clothes. Cassie went straight up to him, giving him no chance to dodge her, like when she had hit him hard in the chest with a double-handed backhand, that first occasion on the court. Before he could back off, she held him and kissed him on the cheek below the left eye, the same place where the ball had hit him as it re-bounded off his chest. "Please, Andy, we need to talk," she whispered in his left ear.

Andy could feel all the eyes on him, not just the Bleakleys and Penny, but all the tennis players seated around.

"Take me bushwalking tomorrow. I promise I won't spoil the day. To Virgin Rock, to the famous lookout."

He hesitated, then realised he had a convenient excuse. "Sorry. I can't. I've promised my dad I'll climb Mt.

Serecold with him. I'm leaving early tomorrow and taking my rock climbing gear. It's likely to be a tricky ascent."

"Is it dangerous, the climb?" The concern—strained, yet obvious.

"Life is dangerous, in many different ways. You must know that!" He was half applauding himself, seeing the hurt in her eyes. "I can't let my father down!"

Streuth, she thought, *you're letting me down! You bloody bugger!* While knowing she had no right to think that way. She looked down, ready to kick his tennis bag, throw his racquet into the crowd. The energy wasn't there. She melted. Tears impossible to hold back.

She moved away, wiped her eyes with a tissue Marg offered, and put her sunglasses back on.

"Come Andrew, sit down, and have tea with us," Fred said. "Tell us the latest on the geography project."

"It's going well, but really I can't stay." He picked up his tennis bag and racquet, turned away and left.

When Fred heard the Suzuki start up, he said to the two teary ladies sitting opposite him. "Blimey, that was a bit rude."

"It's as Penny said, Cassie, he needs time. Come, let's go home to 'The Blockhouse'," Marg said, gathering her hat and purse.

Skye Mattingly saw them as the Bleakleys drove past Gregory Park with Cassandra in the back seat. She guessed they might have been to the tennis centre where Andy would have been playing—Cassie hoping to speak to him. She thought back to her geography teacher's mood. His deliberate manner, when presenting the virtual field trip. He'd been so switched on. So focused that she wondered if he had been faking it. Acting the professor, rather than being his own relaxed self. Hiding an emotional turbulence inside. The Alvarez revelations must be eating away at him. She wanted to console him, provide some comfort. She knew it was an improper thought, a teen girl, and a teacher. It was not her place. Yet, yet! She silently wished this Cassandra Alvos, the Miss Connie Alverez, had never shown up in Comet Downs. *Who, indeed, she thought, is suicidal now?*

The phone rang at 10:30 p.m. at the Goodman's garage as Angie Goodman was locking up. She had expected a call from Seb, asking to be picked up from the rugby clubhouse do—the annual end of season binge where she hoped Seb and his mate, Guy, had obeyed their parents' directives to stay off the grog. It was not Seb but the local police sergeant, David Gower.

"Hi, Angie, I have Seb in the lockup with Guy Lambert. Can you come and collect him? Will explain when you get here. I've just phoned Gwen Lambert."

Sergeant Gower greeted the two angry mothers and explained why the boys were locked-up, as he said, "For their own good!"

The evening had commenced with a sausage sizzle and drinks for the boys in the junior teams. By 8:30 p.m., most of the families with young ones had left. Constable Jones was on duty at the event when a brawl broke out. Seb and Guy were lashing out physically at two older boys who were boasting about vandalising notices around the town—notices about some 'do' coming up at the state school. The constable, with help of club officials, broke up the brawl and then decided the best action was to get the two younger boys out of there and back to the police station.

It was easy for Angie and Gwen to sign the paperwork and take their sons home. But they wanted more from the police sergeant and rang Andy Thomas, begging him to come to the police station and put a case for 'police protection'—not just for their 15 year old boys, who would be scolded and penalised at home for their stupidity, but for the event that they were defending, the right to publicise and gather peacefully. The need to avoid a 1998 St. Matthew's Day incident, that was the imperative, stop any little incidents leading to something much more nasty.

Sunday, 11 September 2016

In the morning, Andy Thomas drove out to meet his father in Consuelo Creek valley. It was cool, just 7°. His brain was spurred on by the freshness. He was indeed a morning person. Late, after 11 p.m., at the Rainworth Downs police station, he had heard Guy and Seb's story. They had made it known that they were incensed by the roguish attitude of the older boys, displayed by the crude despoiling of the presentation posters.
The one, flashed around, read,

'Smartarse Kiddy Play—Stay Away!'

and another the police had collected read,

'Get Rid of the fu…king clown! —Hunt Streuth out of Town!'

As the goading of Guy and Seb continued, they had resorted to using their fists against the loud-mouthed bigger club members until the police constable had intervened.

Andy stopped off at the Goodman's service station for petrol and told them where he was headed.

It was a little precaution he took when travelling alone. Not surprising neither Angie nor Gary was there, just one of their casual employees. So he drove on mulling things over in his mind.

It seems, Andy thought, *that I am the target of written abuse by some older teens, who have picked up on loose town talk, believing that what they overheard being said in jest, legitimised their own appalling acts of bravado. They would never be bothered to understand the context of an issue.* It was disturbing. Humiliating. It was the disease of the small rural town—loose talk and bravado. It was why education needed to connect and enlighten. Geography well taught, he felt, provided the scoping strategies to break the cycle that perpetuates ignorance.

It's unlikely, he argued to himself, *that the vandalising of the posters was a deliberate attempt to derail the preparation for the geography presentation night? It could be that a couple of families, for different reasons, aren't fully onboard with the event. Many Rainworth Downs families have members employed as mine truck or excavator drivers, which might explain a degree of concern. More water could mean bigger mining companies moving in with megaprojects, forcing the small mines out of business, unable to compete. And Josie Strange, living with her grandmother in a hovel behind a small cafe on the highway where her extended family eke out a meagre living, is from a tradition that simply hates any change. There did not seem to be a core focus for any opposition. And really the project was not proposing the building of a dam, any more than suggesting the re-opening of the old outdoor theatre in the town. It was never going to happen. The proposal was simply an issue for investigation and debate.*

Yet another matter troubled him far more. He had kept it to himself. It was the anonymous attacks through social media. Accusations of politicising his teaching, accusations of bullying his students into becoming radical lefties, claims he would be a dead fish blown up by dynamite if he persisted. What hurt more were the jibes that he was debasing himself by dating the Spanish Moll, that she was a slut, like some Spanish porn star named 'Arena'. That his morality had gone down a sexual drain. Postings on Facebook and Twitter as well as direct to his education department email address.

Andrew's father was waiting when he reached the turnoff into the State Forest. Gary Thomas was photographing the *'Parks and Wildlife Service'* sign that had been deliberately smashed. A large vehicle had rammed into it.

"Nice crisp morning. See any four-wheel drives or mining company vehicles on your way?"

"No! Why?"

"There has been some unauthorised drilling for coal-seam gas in here. I'm not sure which company is behind it. They no doubt want to claim that there are coal lenses that are worth fracking to get the gas out. That would stop any move to have this State Forest here added to the National

Park estate. The mining companies think too large an area of the Central Highlands is already off-limits to them."

"I didn't see a vehicle after I left the highway."

"Good. Let's get going. Want to check any damage or new tracks in the forest scrub, an indication of some clandestine activity, then we can climb the peak. Did you bring some ropes?"

"Yes, just as a precaution."

When they did start the ascent of the peak, it was a steady climb from the valley floor. There was one five metre band of coarse sandstone and conglomerate not far below the summit. Andy chimneyed up via a narrow crevice and set a rope to help his father. Then, it was easy going up an exposed ridge to the trig point on top. They spent a while, taking in the view. North down Consuelo Creek Valley, west to Mt. Hornet and Black Alley Peak, both 300 metres higher than their vantage point, and also south towards the Rewan homestead and stockyards in the Carnarvon Creek valley.

Andy went searching and soon found the climber's log in an aluminum cylinder stored amongst rocks below the trig marker. He opened the folded booklet cautiously in case it was in poor condition, then searched through the small number of entries.

"Well, it seems the last party to climb up here was in June 1997, and it included David Gower and Les Smallbone from Rainworth Downs and the manager from Rewan Station police horse stud."

"That doesn't surprise me. Les was quite adventurist before his accident and Gower was a young fit Constable back then. Did they write any notes?"

“Yes, it reads, ‘*Not a difficult climb. Fantastic winter’s day. Great views. Located the aboriginal gallery and multiple burial sites in the sandstone cliffs near two spring-fed waterholes at 423496. Grahame Walsh had discovered the site in 1982 when he lived at Takarrakka’*.”

“Walsh did a lot of exploration and wrote his three books about art sites and scenic wonders in the Carnarvons, but you know all that.”

“Yes. Still the art and burial sites in this this area are interesting.”

“My guess is that it’s one of the locations where the people of the indigenous clans were herded and shot, following the attacks on white settlers at Hornet Bank and Cullin-la-Ringo. The massacre by the whites far exceeded the attacks by the aborigines at those two properties. Australian historians have paid little attention to the frontier wars in Queensland in the 19th century.”

“It makes sense. This secluded area, a small, eroded anticline confined by the hills, was surely just the place to trap the aboriginal warriors and rid the land of its original owners.”

“That’s my assumption. We’ll never find the proof. The history buried with the warriors, their women folk and children as well. They would have been Kongabula or Garingbal people—clans still fighting for Native Title rights. Let’s have morning tea while we enjoy the view like Smallbone’s party would have done. I brought a thermos and cake your mother baked. Then, we can climb down and search for the art site. Should be easy to find having the grid reference and Consuelo topo sheet. While we relax, you can fill me in on 'The Spanish Girl'."

Andy told his father about the outburst of anger by Cassie Alvos at the Mt. Warrinillla factory site, confessing that it was wrong, and a betrayal of trust, to take her there. Then, he explained about the visit of the mother and sister and the reason given for secrecy. He didn't explicitly mention Connie's suicide attempt. Or the trolls using social media to provoke him.

"Well, I'm ahead of you, I think," his father confessing to some enquiries he'd made in tennis circles.

"She is Consuela Alvarez, right? At 12, the 2004 under 14 State tennis champion. A young star at the time. I was still taking you to play in the under 18 competitions, so saw her play a match. It's true Gavin Davis was her coach for a while. I'm told her mother is remembered in tennis circles more than the girl because she was a striking beauty who lit up the stands with her elegance and artistic dress sense."

"Lorae Martinez is still attractive, like her two daughters. The older sister is Alana, unmarried like Consuela."

"What a coincidence about the name. Consuela and Consuelo. That Spanish name means 'solace' or 'a comforting nature'. There's irony in that if I am right that in this enclosed valley below us is a mass murder site. The tribesmen wouldn't have had much of a chance against the guns of the squatters' men and the native police."

"It helps explains Uncle Barry's emotional ties to this upper Comet River area. This is where his ancestral spirits lie. For him it's like our Kokoda, without the ultimate victory."

"He's a great man, Barry. He hides his anger, but the resolve to seek justice is ever present in his dealing with the white man. With us who hold the power."

Adrian Mattingley liked to tease his young sister. Rocky Grammar had finished the third term a week earlier than the state schools, and he had arrived back home by train the day before. When Skye sat down for breakfast that morning, he was quick to shock her.

"Two of your classmates spent time in prison last night. You might be next. Get yourself in a punch-up, defending your geography master, Streuth Thomas. Your heartthrob, I believe."

"That'll do, Adrian," his father was curt with him. "Retract what you just said and apologise to Skye."

Adrian mumbled a response. "Sorry… But I'm right about Guy Lambert and his mate, Seb Goodman, being in the lockup for a couple of hours."

"Excuse me," said Skye to her parents. There was a savage look for Adrian, "I'm Mister Thomas' student not his girlfriend!" She stood and went straight back to her room to check the talk on Twitter and Snapchat. In less than five minutes, she had the details—*the brawl at the rugby club function. Unclear what had motivated Guy and Seb. The mothers and then Mister Thomas called to the police station. No one thought Sir was in trouble with the police. Maybe, the presentation evening could be called off by the police. Too much friction in the town.* She knew Andrew's mobile number and tried phoning him. Then, when there was no connection, she realised he was bushwalking with his dad and unlikely to have reception. She might try later in the day, aware it was inappropriate for her to make a personal call to her teacher. She rang Guy Lambert instead and received his story firsthand.

"It's okay," Guy said, "Seb got a black eye, but it hardly shows on his dark skin, and I have a sore ear and bruised knuckles. We both landed some good punches, but they were taller and stronger. Seb and I are now under '*police protection*'. How about that? And the sergeant is arranging for extra police to be around at our practice next Saturday and at the do Saturday night. Our mums and Mister Thomas were given that assurance. It'll all turn out fine. Seb and I are on community service duties for four hours today, so I've got to go and report in."

It was close to sunset, as Andrew drove back along the Consuelo Creek Road. He was squinting, finding it somewhat difficult to see, because of the sun in his eyes until the road swung towards the northeast. With his father, they'd found the small art gallery, some carvings, and five burial sites still intact with the skeletons wrapped in bark and pushed into crevices high up on the cliffs. Two of the skeletons were small, obviously the remains of young children. It seemed remarkable that the tube burials were still in place given the likely foraging of animal predators, and the scavenging by human artefact hunters. His father had made notes and photographed the gallery and burial sites for his records. "More evidence in support of National Park status for the State Forest remnant," he had said.

Andy made out the cloud of dust, travelling at speed towards him just as his mobile phone rang. He slowed the Suzuki to move to the left verge of the road and stop in order to let the monster truck pass. He daren't look at who was calling as the huge mass of the truck loomed before him.

Instinctively, he ducked sideways. That was the last he remembered.

When he had not returned from Consuelo Creek by 10 p.m., his house mates had sent out a call for information. By then, Andy was in a RACQ rescue helicopter on route to Roma Hospital, suffering concussion, whiplash, broken ribs, cracked pelvis, and a possible ruptured spleen.

Chapter 10

Monday, 12 September 2016

Early on the Monday, the Bleakley's received a phone call from their grandson, Josh Gibson, with news of the crash on the Consuelo Road. A month before Josh had taken a job, working as the assistant vet at the Rewan horse stud and was headed back there just on sunset after playing tennis on Saturday and spending time with family in Rainworth Downs on the Sunday.

"Hi, Josh, why the call? We saw you here just yesterday for lunch. Is anything wrong?"

"I've got some bad news. There was an accident on the Consuelo Valley road. I came across the wreckage driving back to Rewan. Streuth's Suzuki was a crumpled mess. He was lucky, the seat belt must have held him as it summersaulted into the ditch beside the road. Andy was unconscious and in a bad way, not breathing, but I found a pulse and pulled his head back to stop him choking to death. I couldn't get him out of the wreckage by myself to lie him on the ground. So I was ecstatic when I heard a few audible breaths, thank the lord! I pulled out my mobile and found I had a signal. One bar. It was enough. I rang triple zero and gave the location and victim details and waited. The RACQ

Care Flight chopper found us by search light about 9 p.m., with me still supporting Andy's head."

"Blimey Josh. How terrible. Lucky you found him in time."

"The ambo guys were marvelous. Applied a sedative, cut him out of the wreck, checked his vitals, and had him on board the chopper in 40 minutes bound for Roma Base Hospital."

"Thought I'd call you first because you have Cassandra Alvos there. I gather from the talk they are pretty sweet on each other. It's so obvious at tennis, how they smile, hold hands, and whisper."

"Thanks, Josh, for calling. We'll speak to Cassie. You must be buggered. Take care yourself."

"Yes pa! I'll call the principal at the school shortly and give him the sad news."

"Sit down," Fred directed as Marg and Cassie walked into the kitchen. "I have some brandy if you need it."

"Whatever for, Fred?"

Then, he told them about the phone call from Josh.

Connie's immediate thoughts were not about Andrew, but rather her suicide attempt. How the world had betrayed her. How life was cruel! Unbearable! But you were captured in a physical body that instinctively wanted to keep living. And somehow, that thought soothed her. Gave her hope. Gave her belief, no matter how bad he was injured, Andrew Thomas' body would win the battle for survival.

Adrian broke the news in the Mattingley household. His information had come third hand from Sam Goodman, via a school bus driver going out on his morning pick-up. The driver's son had been a good mate of Adrian's in his younger days in the town. "Not sure how accurate it is, but they say Streuth nearly died at the crash scene. Apparently, it was a single vehicle crash. He rolled his Suzuki off the road into a ditch. Might have swerved to avoid a kangaroo and lost control. He's in hospital in Roma, transported by a Care Flight helicopter."

Penny raced to her daughter and took her in her arms. Skye was bellowing. She couldn't control the explosions inside her—her body shaking with anger, the terror of it all flooding her brain. Penny couldn't help crying a little either. "Be brave, Skye, there's a good chance he's quite okay. I'll phone the hospital later for some news."

She couldn't say what she wanted to say, that the person she loved most outside of family might be dying. Instead, she took an easier route. "This ruins everything! The project. The presentation. Everything the class has worked for!"

"Yes, dear. But it's not the end. It's a setback. You can deal with it. Go to your room and have a good cry. You can miss the first period at school today. Find a way to gather yourself together, then arrive at morning recess. Everyone will know by then. There will be an atmosphere of compassion. Everybody sharing the same horror and hope. Comfort for you."

Penny was right. By the time the students and teachers were arriving at Rainworth Downs School, the town was abuzz with confused reports and conspiracy theories about the accident on the Consuelo Road. The principal, Doug James, delayed the first lesson and called the teachers together to tell them what he knew from official sources and via Josh Gibson.

“We will have to cover Andrew’s classes internally today, and then I will try for relief staff for the remainder of the week. Might have to get someone from Emerald. I’ll speak to the regional director to see if she has some suggestions. I reckon, she owes us a favour. As for the presentation night on Saturday, I want that to go ahead. If any of you can help out, especially with setting up the hall and the rehearsal on Saturday, it would be appreciated. I’ll call the Year 10 students together at morning recess and tell them what I’ve told you. We all need to reassure them that we have our utmost confidence in them.”

Merle Gibson silently chastised herself. She had heard talk about a threat on Andrew Thomas’ life. It came via her neighbour, Gina Priddle, wife of the Pungana South electrician. At the time, the rumour had her blessing. She liked the concept of silencing Andrew. He had all these new teaching strategies, using iPads, GIS on computers, fancy projectors, electronic white boards, something called a Swivl that tracked you in the classroom and recorded the lesson. She had taught her way for 20 years, using books and chalkboards. Taught all of Andrew’s year 10 students in a combined Grade 4 and 5—all except Mandy, the vet’s daughter, and Jonathan, the bank manager’s son, who were newer in town. They had all become proficient with reading and writing, punctuation and grammar, basic mathematics, art and craft work, even dear half-blind Josie. Others before them had done very well, like her nephew, Josh, now a vet; or Adrian Mattingley, a top student at Rocky Grammar; and of course the town’s own Country and Western star, Sonny Thorton. If she had her way, it would be absolutely back to basics in the classroom.

Now, she would have to offer her help with this Saturday night shindig. Since her nephew had been on the spot to save Andrew, the least she could do was pitch in and assist with art materials for the Year 10 class displays. And she had an idea for some of Year 7 and 8 girls to get involved, the ones who attended the local ballet classes. She would talk to Gwen Lambert and Angie Goodman. Add a delightful item to stop the evening becoming over formal and possibly downright boring.

Half an hour later, Sergeant Gower had Sam Goodman on the phone exchanging details. "I would like you to recover the wreck with your tow-truck ASAP. Pick up Barry Brownlea and take him with you. Constable Adams is already out there, taking photographs. Get Barry to read the tyre tracks and other evidence of what really happened. Be sure Adams writes thorough notes before you move the wreckage. Then, bring it back here to the police yard."

Chapter 11

Tuesday, 13 September 2016

"Where am I?" Andrew Thomas asked his mother with a grimace, the nauseating pain began in his left hip and travelled up through his ribs to his shoulder. Any move was agony.

"Roma Hospital. You were in an accident. Your Suzy's a write off, but you're going to be okay."

"What day is it?"

"Tuesday late morning. You've been sedated most of the time over the two days. The doctors and nurses have been excellent. You'll have a great deal of pain to endure as you heal. You're on a drip to provide sustenance till you feel ready to eat. Just rest for now. We can talk more when you feel stronger."

Janise Thomas bent over and kissed her son's forehead. "Good to see you awake and alive."

In her lunch break, Cassandra headed to the Comet Hair Salon to make an appointment. Gwen Lambert had just finished with her last customer for the morning and had stopped for a very welcome coffee and sit down.

"Can you fit me in for a trim on Friday morning? Early as possible please?" Cassie inquired.

"Is 8 a.m. okay. My first customer is normally at nine, but I can make a concession."

"Thanks, Gwen. I hope the Bleakleys will bring me in and then maybe take me to Roma. It's my rostered day off."

"Well you'll want to look your best, visiting Andrew in hospital. Terrible business. I've heard from Sam and Angie Goodman that there was definitely a big truck involved. Looks like Andy was hit head on, and the culprit just drove away. Sam Goodman went out with a police constable and Uncle Barry Brownlea to recover the wreck. I believe Barry studied all the tyre marks and vegetation damage and has a very good idea about what happened. The sergeant wants it to be all hush-hush, but in this town that's a difficult request."

"Thanks, Gwen, Marg and Fred are keeping me informed."

"Well, you hang in there. I think Andrew will need you."

And you don't know how much this lady, Connie Alvarez, needs him, Cassie said to herself in her thoughts, as she walked back to the bank.

"I can see the wonder in your faces," Fred Bleakley said when he entered the Year 10 geography class that morning. "Mister James requested me to come because I still have my Queensland teacher's registration, and he wanted someone who understood the project you're working on and knows the sensitivities of the town's history."

"Welcome, Mister Bleakley, Sir," Guy spoke up for the class in his most manly voice. "You are jolly old Fred or Mister B to many of us and Santa at Christmas parties. May we call you Fred in class?"

“Still the smart guy, Master Andrews. I’m only here for this 90-minute session and again for your Thursday class, so I guess that ‘*Fred*’ is okay for those of you who forget it should be ‘Sir’. Just in class mind you. So how’s the project going? All you’re planning? New finds?”

They all looked around wondering who should lead. When Skye remained silent, Jenny Grant spoke up. “The Environmental Impact Study Skye brought back from the library at ‘The Blockhouse’ is a cool resource for our study, really. Today, we need to get copies of various sections of it and distribute them to our work groups. That’s so the slides for our presentation can be prepared using relevant information from that report.”

“Jonathan is investigating the way to create an interactive map of the valley, using GIS overlays to add detail to the map on the screen. It’s very clever.” Seb’s and others’ pleading looks encouraging Jonathan to fill in more detail.

Circumspectly, the technology student contributed. “I’ve also found a Warrinilla 1:100,000 wetland map that covers the Comet River from Lake Nuga Nuga to almost where it meets the MacKenzie River. It’s a digital map I’ve been able to download, and it shows all the many important wetlands, palustrine, lacustrine, and riverine systems. A big concentration of the important habitats around where Carnarvon Creek joins Brown River, and downstream from the Kogabula Scrub around Lake Brown. Over 40 waterbird species are listed for the area. None are rare, though.”

“Well, first of all, we should make sure all the class understands those words Jonathan used,” Fred said in his teaching manner of old. “I’ll write them on the white board.”

“Palustrine?”

“Shallow vegetated swamps,” Mandy was quick with an answer.

“Like Bogarella Lagoon, just off Carnarvon Creek, and Lake Brown now it’s silted up,” Jenny Grant added.

“Lacustrine?”

“Lakes and dammed river channels, like Lake Nuga Nuga, where the water is generally deeper,” came the answer from Grace and Danielle, two of the quieter female students.

“Riverine?”

“River channels and deep ponds along a stream. Where we can go fishing or swimming.” Guy put in.

“Platypus habitat,” Skye said, brightening up considerably. “But the study of aquatic life in the Comet found no platypuses.” Emphasising a plural form and causing a snigger from the boys. It was somewhat un-lady like for Skye, and she immediately regretted it. Blushing, she continued, “And a limited occurrence of freshwater turtles using similar habitats shows that what is left of the riverine ecology is precious.”

“Good to see you are so well-informed.” Fred added his compliments, ignoring Skye’s sexual pun.

“Sir,” Jonathan was quick to arrest attention again, “The wetland map also indicates large areas near the river and along the ana-branches that are remnant wetland ecosystems with 1–50% mosaic coverage of marsh. Some of these areas have been drained sufficiently to be cultivated. I'll be able to project this map as a Power Point slide and one of the class can add comments."

"Any endangered species? Preserving the habitat of the rare lung fish in the Mary River had a lot to do with stopping the Mary River Dam proposal last decade." Fred Bleakley asked, checking their knowledge.

"There is the rare Forrest's mouse in the Riverine forest that is endangered. Forrest with a double 'r'. Named after some naturalist. There's an endemic species of the Ooline tree in the Kongabula scrub. It resembles a half bark eucalypt, but it's not—a very different plant genera." Jenny offered smartly.

Guy chipped in again, "It has been shown that dams and weirs in the Fitzroy system, result in a serious decline in fish stocks down stream. Yellowbelly, catfish, eels, and redclaw have become scarce."

"Looks like you've gathered a great deal of good information. So get on with mocking up your Power Point slides. I'll just circulate and help where needed. Mister Thomas will be very proud of your efforts, and I'm sure the community will be most impressed."

The class settled to work in the groups previously arranged amongst them while Fred Bleakley mused about how education was changing, and how he should revisit '*Ted Talks*'—the T.V. show where he had watched some inspiring presentations about the future of education.

Towards the close of the class session, Skye, still fretting, motioned to Fred for a private word. "Can we tell them any more about the accident to Mister Thomas? They know he's in Roma hospital. Is there an update on his condition?"

"Skye, there is an investigation. It may not exactly have been an accident. I can't say any more. There's a lot of speculation, as you probably know. Andy's okay. Broken pelvis, cracked ribs, damaged spleen, causing some internal bleeding which will all heal. Concussion, but no serious brain injury, it seems. That's what I've heard from his father."

"Do you think the presentation night should have been called off?"

"Definitely not! And Mister James is adamant. That's why I'm here, to help you get it all together."

"Well, can I make an announcement about the practice for Saturday?"

"Attention class. Stop your work. Skye has an announcement." Fred was pleased his old school manner worked with the class, wondering what would be the case in other circumstances, when the motivation to be alert and responsive wasn't there.

Skye straightened her uniform and spoke in her authoritative school captain's voice. "Mister James has arranged for all of us who are presenting on Saturday night to have two coaching sessions in public speaking. That's tomorrow and Thursday afternoons at 3 p.m. for an hour each time. All day Saturday from 9 a.m. till about 3 p.m. we'll be setting up our display and practicing for the presentation at night. The music group, involving Mandy and Jane, are rehearsing two choral items helped by Misses. Jones, the visiting music teacher. Jane's cousin, Sonny Thornton, will be in town and will be playing guitar, as he sings with a backing group of girls. I know how a lot of you girls and your mums and cousins think Sonny's a bit of a heartthrob, so you should enjoy that part of the evening."

Sergeant Gower had read Constable Adams' report and spoken with Sam Goodman and Barry Brownlea. It was time to call the district superintendent in Emerald, yet he hesitated. The presence of investigating detectives in the town would cause an almighty ruckus that he didn't want prior to the school function on Saturday night. For sure, there would be rumour and speculation, but an overt investigation meant someone in the community was likely to be charged with dangerous driving, if not attempted murder. He knew there was a need for a statement from Andrew Thomas, anything he remembered about the crash. He could contact the superintendent in Roma. *They could do a police interview at Andrew's bedside when he is well enough, without showing my suspicions about intentional foul play.*

Wednesday, 14 September 2016

Midmorning on the Wednesday, the duty doctor at Roma base Hospital, stood with a nursing sister beside the bed of patient 121C, Andrew Charles Thomas, allowing him to listen to their conversation. They both knew from the patient's chart that the vital signs had been checked several times, and there were no critical concerns. "Sister, the drip can be removed, Andrew can be on normal meals from now on while he's with us. X-Rays show the spleen is punctured but not badly enough for Andrew to be sent to Rockhampton for splenectomy. We've sealed off the bleeding. You are very lucky, young man. You took a severe blow to your head, but there appears to be no lasting brain injury. Your broken pelvis will heal slowly. You'll be unable to bear weight on your left leg for at least a month. Your ribs will also heal themselves. You are in for a lot more pain and discomfort, but we'll monitor that and supply painkillers. Right, Sister, he's in your hands. The police want to get a statement from him as soon as he feels well enough. Perhaps this afternoon."

Andrew's parents visited him in the hospital on the Wednesday evening, pleased to see him wide awake. He told them what the doctor had said and that he had given a statement to the local police sergeant. "I said I saw the monster truck speeding towards me in a cloud of dust, so I pulled to the side of the road for it to pass. Nothing after that except the impact and a sense of flying then falling trapped in a cage. Was my phone found at the crash site?"

"Yes, I have it here in my handbag. Josh Gibson, who found you in the wreck, and kept you breathing till the Care Flight arrived, recovered it and had it passed on to us. I suppose you want to check your incoming calls."

"I have a feeling it rang just before the truck hit me. I keep hearing the ring tone in my head then the explosion of the crash. Thanks, I'll check it later."

"The police suspect it was deliberate, not an accident," Gary Thomas revealed. "They sent Barry Brownlea to inspect the site and vehicle tracks and that's Barry's opinion."

"If that's true, any ideas who?"

"The perpetrator may not be the real villain. Just acting for some other party. Mining or gas companies, perhaps, or just someone believing it was his duty to silence the town 'greenie'. Who knows. I'm sure there will be an investigation by police detectives."

Janise Thomas was anxious to change the subject. Not dwell any more on the accident. "Guess who took your Year 10 geography lesson, yesterday?"

Andy thought for a while. "Maybe Mister James, the principal."

"It was Fred Bleakley," she said. "Good old Fred."

"So the presentation night is going ahead with Fred helping?"

"James had said your accident was a good reason to keep it going. Told all his staff they had to get behind it. I think they were surprised he was so decisive."

"And Fred said the students are marvelous. So well informed and organised," Gary added.

"You needn't worry. It's all under control. Pity you won't be there."

When his parents had left, Andy checked his phone. There were many text messages expressions of sympathy and best wishes. He skipped through them. For some reason, the ringing in his head was demanding he determine who had called just ten or so seconds before the wipeout. It was voice mail. *'I've heard about last night and the call to the police station. Hoping you're okay, and you weren't in trouble like Guy and Seb. See you at school tomorrow.'* He couldn't mistake the fluttering voice—it was Skye Mattingley.

Thursday, 15 September 2016

During the Thursday geography class workshop, Fred Bleakley showed his delight with the progress. The display posters being prepared covered geology; comparative stream flow figures in the Fitzroy system; flood reports and photos from 2010–11; an annotated large map of the wetlands along the river; bird photos from the Stanley Sturgess' collection; and a computer setup with directions for viewers to play the ABC Landline program about irrigated farming filmed at the Stevens farm. He watched while Skye rehearsed her speech, and was shown how it could be recorded using the latest Swivl device. The same technology, he was told, that Mister Thomas used to record his formal lessons and package them with a link on the school website so the students could review them at home. Another surprise for Fred was that the white board transformed into an interactive touch screen with the Comet River Valley map projected on it. It was child's play, indeed, to use it, and he was both dumbfounded and amused when introduced to how it works by the vision-impaired young Josie.

Skye confronted her mother that evening. "I won't be able to see Mister Thomas till Sunday when it's all over, and I'm on holidays. Will you take me?"

"Of course, Skye, both your father and I. We know how badly you want that. Remember you are his student, nothing more. You don't have priority over others who may like to visit and wish him well."

Skye wiped a tear from her eye. No point in hiding her emotions now.

"I practiced my introductory speech today, during the public speaking practice."

"How did it go?"

"The workshop leader suggested some changes to improve the effect. He explained how I could strengthen the tone without shouting into the mike. I hadn't understood until he demonstrated how shouting into a microphone causes sound distortion. I was asked to present my piece several times in front of the others to emphasise what he meant about the emphasis in the delivery."

"Guy, Jenny, Jane, and Mandy will all trial their presentations in the hall Friday morning. Seb is a bit of a worry, but Grace and Danielle are going to help him explain the indigenous viewpoint while projecting some Power Point slides. Mister Bleakley suggested that we needed photographs of the best artefacts in 'The Blockhouse' indigenous collection. He promised he'd get Cassie to take them."

"I'll help on Saturday morning if it's needed. So can Adrian. It will do him good to help. But I'll go to tennis in the afternoon to thank Josh Gibson if he's there. You know he found the crash, called triple zero, and waited three hours for the CareFlight helicopter to arrive, holding Andrew's head up and keeping him breathing while unconscious. If there's a hero in this dreadful business, it's Josh."

"You'll have to thank and praise him for me." Skye insisted. Then added, "I mean for all the geography class."

When Gareth and Penny Mattingley read the draft of Skye's presentation, they could sense how much it all meant to her, this whole project.

'We wish to begin by paying our respects to the local indigenous peoples, elders past and present and their descendants. Uncle Barry Brownlea is here to begin the night with his Welcome to Country.

When Mister Thomas started us on this project, we, our class, didn't know about the history of previous proposals to build a dam on the Comet and tame the river. We were all born this century so... Though many of you adults know about the investigations by SunWater and the Department of Natural Resources in the 1990s that led to the Starlee site being chosen, we were all uninformed until we started this 'Fake News' study project. Other sites in the Fitzroy River system were also investigated by SunWater during the 1960s, resulting on the Fairbairn Dam being constructed on the Nagoa in 1972. The Nathan Gorge Dam on the Dawson River, also planned back in that era, is still awaiting government funding.'

They both read on for another page then came to the sign off piece.

'Thank you for coming. We hope you have enjoyed our presentation and go away better informed. A Queensland Senator, the Minister for infrastructure development in Central and North Queensland, recently delivered a speech, promoting the benefits of more dams on the Fitzroy. Now, you have listened to our presentations and taken a look at our displays, you should be better informed. We, who have been involved in this research, suggest to the Rainworth Downs community, that while perhaps supporting dams

elsewhere, you should say 'NO' at this time to a dam on the Comet. Let our river run free.'

"Do you think," Gareth asked Penny, "That Skye is setting herself up for derision? Some quarters are always ready to criticise the tall poppy. Spread some gossip."

"You're possibly right. Her own brother has already had a go at her, so it's likely others are sniffing around for something to gossip about."

"We might need to think of a lifebuoy strategy after this is over."

"Don't you mean life-girl?" Penny quipped, slapping Gareth on the jaw, as he took her into his arms and kissed her in return.

Chapter 12

Friday, 16 September 2016

Gareth Mattingley took Adrian with him on an early morning visit to the crash site on the Consuelo Creek road. He wanted to be absolutely sure, as the Shire Engineer, that the road conditions hadn't contributed to the crash. After they looked around, Adrian said, "It's pretty obvious that Andrew pulled over to the edge of the built-up bank and was hit at a speed which tumbled him with the Suzuki into the ditch."

But Gareth had some doubts. "What we have to consider is that Andrew might have had the sun in his eyes. He would have only been conscious of a huge swirling mass rushing towards him from the other direction. What if he was distracted by something, such as a call on his mobile?"

"If we have access to his phone we can check that. We could ask Josh Gibson. He was the one who found the crashed Suzuki with Andrew on death's door. Mum plays tennis with Josh tomorrow afternoon. Get her to ask him about Andrew's phone—if he found it?"

"Remind me tomorrow, Adrian. Look here at the tracks, the truck has skidded briefly in the gravel, suggesting slowing but not stopping. The driver would have felt the crash and, big as it might have been, there would be some damage to the front end of the vehicle."

"It was a mine truck, super big tyres."

"Yes, stolen from the Pungara South mine and still missing."

"No reports on where it is?"

"Gary Thomas, Andrew's father, says the police and the mining company should look in the State Forest that is off this road 20 km up below Mt. Serecold. He says there has been some illegal exploratory drilling in there over the past few months. Some vandalism and new vehicle tracks.

He had Andrew with him checking that out on Sunday, and Andrew was driving back here while Gary went home to Roma the way he would have come in, via Rewan horse stud."

"Should we go and look in this State Forest?"

"Not today, Sergeant Gower doesn't want to stir things up any more till after the school show is over tomorrow night. But I'd bet he already has the Rewan and Consuelo Station staff looking into it."

The Bleakleys were on their way to Roma with Connie Alverez when her phone rang. After taking the call, she announced, "There is a bomb scare at the Rainworth Downs School, and the children had been moved out to the playing fields for safety while the school is being searched. That was Claudia with the news."

"Streuth!" exclaimed Fred as he scrutinised the road ahead for rogue kangaroos. "Sorry, that's not the appropriate word in these circumstances."

"*La consternación*, a similar Spanish expression of dismay."

"The year 10s will be fuming," Fred commented. "Mister James had cancelled their formal lessons for the day, so they could practice their presentations and finish the display posters."

"There's surely not a bomb," Marg added. "Just a hoax. Someone opposed to the presentation night being deliberately obstructional."

While the Breakleys sat and talked with Andrew at his bedside, Janise Thomas took the opportunity to get to know 'The Spanish Girl'.

"My husband tells me your real name is Consuela Alverez. Is that right?"

Consuela was nervous, anxious to be accepted, to be put at ease as a friend. Janise was imposing, not in size but in conviction. It showed in the manner of speech, in her penetrating gaze, and the way she clutched her handbag.

"Yes. There were some reasons for hiding my family name. There's a legal inquiry into some abuse that happened in my teen years. I am not permitted to reveal more at this time. Please understand I don't want to be secretive."

Consuela feared it was the beginning of an inquisition. An examination of her morals, her possible past indiscretions, her purpose of befriending Andrew, her future intentions. She answered as honestly as she dared without mentioning her suicide attempt, something she wished had never happened. She knew that before the end of the year it could become public news, even in Roma.

After her questioning had finished, Janise went on with a concerned vigour.

"You know, don't you, that Andrew is devoted to his teaching career. If he ever married, it would need to be someone who shared that passion."

"Andrew and I are friends. We are just getting to know each other. We share some common interests—the natural environment, tennis. I feel comfortable in his presence."

"I hear you put on a hysterical turn at Lake Nuga Nuga. He was distraught about that."

"He has good reason to feel that way. I am here to apologise to him personally. Please allow me to do that. Alone with him. I'm not here to steal his heart."

At his hospital bedside, Consuela gave Andrew a personalised get well card with a photo of two brolgas dancing. "Taken on our first outing," she reminded him.

He examined the card, admired the photo, and read her cheery words. *'Signed Consuela XXX'*.

"Take a seat," he said, saying nothing more in welcome.

Consuela waited. She examined the patient for signs of distrust or rejection hidden within the repeated grimaces of pain.

"Please, take my hand and look at me," she requested.

Another long pause. Then, he offered a compliment, "You look stunning…as always. You've had your hair trimmed. Makes you look more…innocent."

"I'm not innocent, whether you mean 'naive'…or if you imply, 'accused'. I came to apologise for my Nuga Nuga outburst, and to reassure myself that you are going to recover and be the man you desire to be."

"The Bleakleys can fill you in on my injuries and the prognosis for healing on your drive home. I must ask how are you coping? Are you on medication?"

"It was good to have my mother and Alana visit. I believe they explained my history to you. They are an important part of my healing team. Physically you should heal relatively quickly. I'm counselled that mental illness takes a great deal longer."

Andrew was silent again, so she went on, "Dear Marg and Fred have helped me understand…how to acknowledge the oval-shaped carvings as symbolic, not in any way crude. I will get over that phobia I displayed at Nuga Nuga. The fact is, you now know I am a damaged soul in other ways. I am still on some anti-depressant medication. We'll have to talk about it another time, if you really want to continue a relationship."

"Yes, I'd like that," Andrew admitted sheepishly.

She considered the answer. "Does that mean we are still friends for now?"

Andrew nodded, a cheesy grin delivered with difficulty.

"You should know your mother has made it clear I'm not the right partner for you. I'll understand if you want to cut me out of your life. Yet I might not give in easily."

"She's a paper tiger, my mum, you'll see."

"Last night, I photographed aboriginal artefacts in 'The Blockhouse' collection—photos the students can use at the geography class presentation. I'll help with the setting up and finalising the Power Point slides tomorrow. Fred is amazed at their knowledge and application."

"It's good of you to help. I wish I could be there. You can see I'm in a lot of pain, though I'm told everything is healing—the hip, the ribs, the spleen. When I am discharged in a month or two, I'll need crutches for a while."

"You'll also need a new vehicle."

“I’ll miss the Suzy.” Memories from the trip in the Suzuki to Mt. Mooloolong and Cave Hill filled her mind. That lovely day. It was then when Consuela felt ready to cry and let it all gush out, yet composed herself. “I can see you need to rest. I’ve overstayed the time. The nurse said ten minutes, maximum.”

She gave Andrew’s right hand a squeeze. Then stood, bent across him to kiss him gently on the lips. “Just so you remember I was here,” she said, and left.

On the drive back to Rainworth, the discussion had been about the prognosis for Andrew Thomas’ recovery till Fred turned the conversation to Year 10 geography class presentation night. “You know, in the classroom those two days, I learnt so much more from them than anything I could offer. I bet those boys who roughed up Guy Lambert and Seb Goodman would have been behind the bomb hoax today. Just more spitefulness. If I’m right, due to their naivety, they have aligned themselves with the ultra-conservative voices in the district.”

“From what you say about the students, they’ll take the disruption all in their stride. Much of the town must now be behind them.” Consuela commented.

“The apparent accident, running Andrew off the road, is more sinister,” Fred went on. “There are people in this town who want to be rid of him. They think any environmentalist is a bloody pain in the arse.”

“Fred, you shouldn’t say such things,” Marg interjected to silence him.

Consuela returned to her own thoughts. She wanted to believe the accident was just that. Perhaps, Andrew was distracted by something and made a mistake on the narrow road. She didn't want the complication of foul play, and the worry of who was behind it. That might mean she wasn't safe, perhaps Skye too, as well and his other students. Anyone befriending Andrew might become an easy target.

Adrian Mattingley was having a busy day. It had begun with a promise from Central Fitzroy News at Emerald that they would go to print on a 12-page tabloid as a special edition to be available at the Rainworth Downs State School event on the Saturday night, as long as they could shore up sufficient advertisements to help fill the pages. Adrian was in his second year of media studies at school, and in doing so he had built up a web of contacts with a number of media outlets. Primarily, he had gained the support from his Uncle Glynn, the Editor at The Rockhampton Bulletin, to help make it happen. He promised he'd write a compelling article on the Consuelo Road accident as the lead story and had just completed the first draft when Skye phoned home to tell him about the bomb scare. "Just give me 20 minutes while I do an edit on the draft article for the CF news."

The article read:

Foul Play on the Consuelo Road

'Rumour has it that the local police are convinced the vehicle crash that nearly ended the life of popular Rainworth Downs geography teacher, Andrew Thomas, on the lonely Consuelo Road at around 5:30 p.m. last Sunday, 14 September, was not an accident. Thomas was on his way home from having climbed Mt. Serecold earlier in the day with his father, well-known Roma-based QPWS Head Ranger, Gary Thomas, when his vehicle, a little Suzuki

Jimny, was apparently rammed off the road by a huge mine truck, travelling at speed in the opposite direction.

Evidence from the crash site indicates the Suzy was hit head on the driver's side, as Thomas pulled over to let the offending truck pass. One theory put forward was that Thomas was blinded by the setting sun, but where the crash occurred, he would have actually been travelling northeast and not northwest into the sun. Police have not yet ruled out the possibility that Thomas was distracted by a kangaroo jumping out from the road verge, or maybe by responding to a call on his mobile phone, causing him to temporarily lose control of his vehicle.

Thomas was trapped for three hours in the mangled wreck beside the road till the Care Flight rescue chopper arrived, and the crew cut him out of the wreck. He had been kept alive by the efforts of young vet, Josh Gibson, who came across the wreck just on dark and immediately phoned triple zero. Police believe the other vehicle was a South Pungara coal haulage truck which was stolen on the Sunday morning and is still missing.

Andrew Thomas is in Roma Base Hospital with a broken hip, cracked ribs and ruptured spleen. Doctors say he would have died at the scene if he had not been for the quick thinking of the young vet who was on his way back to Rewan Station where he currently works. Gibson stood beside the wreckage, holding Thomas' head up while the victim was unconscious and likely to choke on his own vomit, all the time, till the emergency services arrived, massaging Thomas' heart in case of the effects of shock. Anyone who has information about the missing truck or who was responsible should contact Crime Stoppers or the Emerald or Roma police.'

Adrian arrived at the school to find the students and teachers out in the open playground while police searched rubbish bins and lockers for any sign of a bomb. He immediately briefed the principal about the newspaper proposal and sought permission to try to make it happen. He then found Skye in a foul mood, disgusted with the delays. He was brief in explaining the newspaper idea as if it was already as unstoppable as a flood from a dam burst.

"Could your class put together three or four articles about the benefits or problems with a dam on the upper Comet. Have one of the English teachers or Misses Gibson, she's the best at spelling and grammar, check the copy. Then get Mister James' approval and have it ready by 4 p.m."

"You're bloody crazy," Skye responded. "We're already flat out getting displays finished and finalising Power Point presentations. We're not fucking journalists as well. Go chase a goanna."

"But you've got loads of information that's going to waste. You can't bloody well cover a quarter of it tomorrow night."

"That's not your problem! It's ours! You assume too bloody much!"

Guy Lambert injected himself between the brother and sister. "Everyone is staring at you two. Little Grade Twos aghast at the swearing." Then, he turned and grabbed Skye's flaying arms. "Calm down, Skye. There could be value in Adrian's proposal, if I've overheard correctly. Four or five of us could be in print, sell our message. Put some other angles forward not covered directly in the presentation."

"It's too fucking rushed. We don't have the time."

"Look. I'll ask around and see if Jenny could write a piece on the economics of a dam project, Mandy will love to write about the birdlife and endangered species. I could get help with the pros and cons of the Warrinilla Dam site. Grace and Danielle can use stuff from the interview they did yesterday evening with Uncle Barry."

"4 p.m. An impossible deadline!"

"Let me worry about that. It's surely worth a try."

"Good thinking, Guy. I'm bloody confident it can happen, but I must get on and hustle local businesses for advertisements. Also, I need to phone the Rocky and Emerald schools that are hoping to attract you guys next year. If I can get my school, Rocky Grammar, to sign up for an ad, I'm sure one or two others like, St. Brendan's at Yeppoon, will follow suit for sure. Might need to add some photos but CF News say they have quite a few already that would be suitable, including one of the school and one of Andrew Thomas. Also, they have some material from a freelance photographer, somebody by the name of Ashdown, who has great photographs and the history of Lake Nuga Nuga on his website."

When the all-clear siren went off, a great cheer of relief went around the grounds like a Mexican wave and there was a rush to get out of the sun and to the toilets.

By 3 p.m., Guy had draft features from Jenny, Mandy, and Danielle to present to Mister James for approval. He himself had lifted extracts from the Starlee Dam Environmental Impact Report to be used to fill space in the newspaper with an appropriate acknowledgment of the source. Skye was the one struggling with what to write. She wanted Fred Bleakley's help, but she knew he'd been visiting Andrew in hospital and would not be home to Rainworth yet. In desperation, she phoned Roma Hospital and asked if she could speak to the patient, Mister Andrew Thomas. Andrew was sleeping when the phone rang. It took a while to orientate himself, to discover a telephone had been installed on the table by his bed.

"Hello," expecting it would be his mother testing that the phone she had arranged for him actually worked.

"Hello, Sir, it's Skye."

"Skye? Does your mum know you're calling?"

She ignored his question. "I needed to know how you are. The class has missed you."

"I'm recovering. I'm having to put up with the pain and soreness. Time will fix everything. It will all heal slowly. I'll be out of here in a month, I hope. I'll need a walking stick for a while. Back at school before mid-term, I expect."

"We want you back as quickly as possible. It would be awful if there were complications during your recovery, and you weren't with us the day we finish the year. It's our send-off from ten years at the school, but you know that. Please get well quickly."

"Well, hey, how's the project going?"

"We have it all planned, and there will be a special edition of the CF News. My brother, Adrian, pulled some strings, helped by our uncle at The Bulletin. Five of us Year 10s are contributing articles."

"That's really great."

"I need your help. Adrian's waiting for an article from me for the back page. Something about the purpose of the project. Why we are messing around with an untruth. With false news."

"It's pedagogy, Skye. Education in the IT age. Creative education. Education that opens your mind to possibilities. Education that avoids a narrow view of intelligence as measured through tests set by academics. Tests thrust on students in order to create statistical tables that rank schools and students in a stereotyped way. It's learning that is open-ended, that helps students discover passions…I could go on. The so called 'dam proposal' was just a ruse to set you on a journey of discovery."

"Can I quote you?"

"Of course."

"Could you send an email saying all that? Send it on your mobile phone. I need it in under half an hour… skyemat@gmail.com."

"Well, I guess I might just manage that if you hang up now. A special effort for the bossy Skye."

"I think you once said to me, 'The Skye's the limit!' I presume you meant Skye's a bugger with her demands? Sorry for pestering you! I love you, Sir. I was desperate!"

"Skye, don't get false ideas. I'm your teacher. Nothing more, remember."

"I'm coming to see you at the hospital on Sunday. I'll have all the news from tomorrow's night's do."

She smiled as she hit the 'end' button on her phone. The world was suddenly a beautiful place again.

Chapter 13

Friday Evening, 16 September 2016

That Friday evening, Les Smallbone went to the Comet Hotel for a couple of drinks before going home. He was joined by Councillor Simon Stevens, while Gareth Mattingley, the local shire engineer, sat aside quietly listening.

"I'm informed that Sergeant Gower is taking no chances with tomorrow's events. Two of the stock squad police have been brought in from Roma, a constable from Emerald and another from Blackwater. Wants to keep everything peaceful and civil."

"Glad to hear that," Smallbone replied as he took a swig of his beer and gave off an audible belch. "This whole geography class thing is causing as much of a stir as the protest in '98. I tried to get it all called off, you both know. Doug James, the principal, wasn't listening. Announced that the accident to young Thomas made it all the more important to go ahead. I thought Doug was a wimp, but I was wrong this time."

"Blimey Les, it's good education! Not just for the kids, but for the whole town. That's the view I've come to seeing the effort my nephew and Gareth's daughter have been putting in. Newer residents who have come in with the mining boom and the young ones born this century know nothing about the Starlee Dam proposal and why it never happened."

"I've been invited tomorrow night, so I'll go along and reserve my judgment."

"Those two lads who roughed up my nephew, Guy, and Seb Goodman, were responsible for the bomb hoax at the school today. One of them is the son of that mad Paddy O'Connor, suspected of being on 'ice'. Gower has laid charges and locked both the lads up to get them out of the way till Sunday."

"Not sure that's a good idea." Gareth Mattingley spoke up. "It could stir up more trouble with the young roughs who will be drinking tonight in the Railway Pub bar. Blokes from the mines and a few stockmen with no wives to go home to. By their third or fourth pot, the talk could get out of hand. Sam Goodman told me he might pop in himself and see what the mood is like. What mischief's in the air, I believe he said."

"Any chance the road conditions contributed to the Thomas accident, Gareth?"

"I went out and had a careful look early today. The gravel is a bit loose, but the road is wide enough for the two vehicles to safely pass. My hunch is the same as Barry Brownlea's. The Suzuki was hit at force front on the driver's side, and it summersaulted into the ditch."

"But if he was driving into the setting sun," Les Smallbone put in. "And was distracted while answering a call on his mobile, it could be all Thomas's fault."

"That doesn't explain why the tracks of the big truck were clearly on the wrong side of the road before and after the collision."

"The truck might have swerved to avoid a kangaroo."

"Really Les, now you're joking. A truckie swerving to miss a kangaroo!"

"Well, maybe Sam Goodman will pick up a clue from the loose talk in the bar," the Councillor suggested. "Andrew Thomas' conservation views are against him in this community."

"My son Adrian has another theory. Whoever wanted to get rid of Andrew did so because of the young woman, Cassandra Alvos. A stunning beauty arrives in town and all the young men get hard-ons and hope they might score, but she only has eyes for one man…Streuth! That's unfair in their eyes. He needed to be eliminated!"

"That's just as much farfetched, Gareth," Les Smallbone protested, and Simon Stevens agreed.

"We may never know, but perhaps it shouldn't be ruled out. If the Suzuki was rammed off the road deliberately, it may have nothing to do with the false news project or the presentation night. All to do, you might say, with 'tribal' law in a bush town. Only one rider is given the chance to ride the best buckjumper at the rodeo, and all the other riders become envious. Another drink? My shout!"

Sam Goodman was not fond of pubs. He drank socially, that was all. Angie's youngest brother, Adam, was more a regular and Sam bought a pot at the bar and joined Adam at a small table.

"Hi, Sam, what brings you here to this maelstrom of iniquities?"

“Still being smart with words, I see. Ebony not with you?”

“She’s at the toilet. We’re about to order a meal. Chef’s special—bangers and chips probably, always delicious. Will you join us?”

“Yes. But I want to stay close enough to hear the rumours or boasting by the FIFO miners.” Then, he lowered his voice to a whisper. “What’s being said about the accident to Streuth and the missing truck?”

“One you serviced?”

“No way. I’m not implicated. It was a monster dump truck, so the police believe, serviced at Blackwater or on site at the mine. Still missing.”

“Electric? Wouldn’t go too far.”

“Pungara South haven’t released more details. Could be an inside job.”

Ebony joined them, singing, “Hello, can you hear me…”

Sam prided himself, that he knew the Adele song. Angie had sung it lovingly to him one morning recently to wake him up.

“Hi, Sam, nice to see you.”

She sat down next to Adam and sipped on her rum and coke, then put an arm around him. She was saucy, but upfront and honest. She suited the more reserved and erudite Adam. “Guess what I just heard?” She leant over towards Sam, suspecting he could be in the pub, phishing for information. Sent to listen in to the swill of conversation.

“That Marilyn chick with the big boobs spilling out, and one of her nightlife mates were in the washroom. They both claim some of the shameless bloody heavies, all muscles and tattoos, usually good for a $200 fuck on Friday nights half way through their eight-day FIFO turnaround, when any bloody pussy will do—they are boasting they are going to jump that Cassie, the parading slut from the bank."

"I suspect Cassandra Alvos is under police protection tonight, though she may not know it."

"They claim they got rid of Streuth, and they are gonna show her what real bloody men can do—pack root her, up the arse as well. Then, make her suck them all off afterwards. Bloody fucking mongrels!"

The horror struck him. If there was truth in it, he would need to phone Sergeant Gower and Fred Bleakley immediately. "Do you know which ones?"

Ebony drew him close and whispered in Sam's ear. "Don't look till you're casually walking by to the gents. The leader is the loud-mouthed Irish stag, balding with a ginger beard. Fucking obnoxious in bed, Marilyn claims. He's called Bluebeard by his ugly mates. He's not the biggest, but the most dangerous prick amongst the rabble."

"Did they reveal when?"

"The tarts didn't suggest that, but you can tell from the sledging and bellowing going on that it could even be later tonight."

"Thanks, Ebony, your Marilyn friend is a terrific Mata Hari. I must go and make some urgent calls. Adam will explain." He drank down the rest of his beer. "Let me know if you hear some more. It may mean nothing. Just drunken boasting, most likely." Sam stood, departing as inconspicuously as possible.

Fred Bleakley was tired. It had been quite a day—the long drive to Roma, two hours at the hospital, a cafe stopover for lunch, then the drive back, including a diversion along Consuelo Road to the accident site—a chance for Cassie to know, to live some of Andrew's pain. Like her, Andy had been plunged so close to death and survived. He and Marg gave her some quiet time.

You think, she thought, standing there beside the ditch, the police flagging marking the spot, *that your life has some purpose, that you are on a mission mapped out for you, though the destination maybe somewhat obscure; and when you paddle the river ahead, it's smooth going until the stream makes an abrupt turn, crashing over cascades, so violently you lose control, caught unprepared. You flounder. You want to scream to the Gods, but it's impossible—caught in the turbulence, the churning. And you know you are drowning. Terror has you for a brief moment, then you accept that this is death... If you survive, re-surface, you cling to a faith that it was meant to be, and that there is a side stream, a distributary you can take. That for better or worse your life continues on with a changed destination.*

Fred showered and was in his pajamas when the phone rang. Before he could answer, a screaming siren burst into his eardrums. Cassie's *Athena* alarm! She had demonstrated it for him and Marg just a week before, protesting that she was safe and it would always be with her when she went across to the ablutions in 'The Blockhouse'. He was out to the back landing headed for the steps when he stumbled over a loose mat, and crashed to the floor. Marg was there in her nightwear as he pushed up onto his knees, cursing. "It's Cassie!" he yelled, "Cassie!!!" But he had lost time and he felt so bloody demoralised—his dentures still in the bathroom.

Three thugs had attacked Cassie. One from behind, yanking her dressing gown off. One tearing at the clothes underneath. A third shouting orders. “Get the fucking bitch to the Ute!”

Cassie fought back, thrashing out, kicking wildly, scratching at arms and faces, trying to break free as the terror rushed through her body. Somehow, she managed to hit the alarm for a second time before they ripped it away. “NO! NO! NOOOO!” She was screeching, screeching, screeching.

The attack was all so quick, the boss one, punching her in the belly and the crutch, a second gaging her, clamping her jaws closed with his massive fist as she tried desperately to bite, bite, bite.

“Get the whore on the ground, you two fucking clowns, and I’ll do her here and now. That will shut the bloody bitch up! Then, we’ll get away. Those bastards at the house will be calling the fucking pigs!”

As Bluebeard dropped his dacks and took his cock out ready to rape Cassie, a police flashlight lit up his erection.

“Bloody fucking hell!” Three voices bellowing into the cold night air as the thugs stared momentarily into the light, then split. One running for the Ute hidden under trees, another one back to ‘The Blockhouse’ with a yelping police dog giving chase. Bluebeard, his pants around his ankles, stumbled forward, hobbled by his own jocks.

“Put your miserable little prick away, Bluebeard! You’re headed to gaol for attempted rape!” Senior Sergeant McLeod from the Stock Squad was calling from the shadows, as his constable grabbed the bastard and quickly applied an armlock. Bluebeard's pathetic response in broken Gaelic, "Go fuck yourself sideways!" hardly rated with the two cops.

The second attacker had reached the Ute to find the engine would not start. McLeod walked casually over. "Good evening, Sir. My, my, it's Patrick O'Connor, his self. Looks like you need a lift to the police station. Fancy joining your son in a police cell? It'll be interesting what you both have to tell the Holy Father at confession tomorrow."

Fred Bleakley knelt beside Cassie, as the siren of Sergeant Gower's paddy wagon could be heard rapidly approaching. "There were three of them bastards," she managed through gritted teeth. "Been attacked before on the street in Rocky, now bloody three of them!"

"It's okay, Cassie. The police are taking care of them. Marg has a clean gown for you. Are you able to stand up?"

"I'm not badly hurt. Not physically, I don't think."

"Come on, then, we'll get you inside the house."

Fifteen minutes later, Sergeant Gower knocked on the front door and Fred let him in.

"That Bluebeard bastard, Cormac O'Brien, and the crazy Patrick O'Connor are safely locked in my van. Sergeant McLeod and his constable have saved the other FIFO guy from the savage dog. It threatened to tear him apart. They'll take him back to Roma, since our cells will be full for a day or two."

"How's Miss Alvos?"

"Marg is seeing to her. Physically okay. Emotionally, she's just coping."

"I'll need a statement from her. Can you bring her to the station in the morning?"

"Yes, of course. If she's up to it."

"Thanks, Fred. We got a tip off via Sam Goodman. Some talk at the Railway pub. Good he was there and called me immediately."

"It may have been Sam phoning here with a warning when Cassie's alarm sounded for the first time. I rushed out and didn't answer."

"You're right, he rang me back worried we'd be too late, but I already had McLeod and his constable patrolling out this way."

"Bloody awful business. Lucky they were so quick to be here."

"It has been important to have the extra police help. See you tomorrow, Fred, with Cassandra."

Chapter 14

Saturday, 17 September 2016

The gathering at the Rainworth Downs school hall the next day included the principal, Doug James, five teaching staff, two teacher aides, eight parents, and all the members of the Grade 10 geography class except Josie. The shy near-sighted student was always dependent on the school bus for transport into Rainworth Downs; and in Andrew's absence, no one had thought to offer to collect her by car till her absence was apparent.

"I'll go and pick her up this afternoon," Merle Gibson offered. It was the type of kindly act she was noted for. "She can have dinner at my place and stay over after the big night. It would be such a disappointment for her if she was left out."

"Thank you, Misses Gibson," the sentiment conveyed by five or more voices.

They all knew what tasks they had to do. Skye, helped by her mother, had prepared a run sheet.

Her brother Adrian was there as well to update them on the special edition of the Central Fitzroy News. The sub-editor was finalising the layout. He suggested he had space for two photos from the working bee, so Adrian began snapping away.

"Where's Cassandra Alvos?" He asked his mother and the other ladies talking over the supper arrangements. "I know she's a much better photographer than I am, and has a better camera as well."

His query was greeted by silence. It was as if four sets of lips were tightly zipped. What wasn't being said? Fred Bleakley would know but where was Fred as well? Skye had said both Fred and Cassie would be helping.

Frustrated, he took ten photos of students and fathers working on setting up the displays. The sub-editor would select a couple, no doubt. The 10 a.m. deadline was approaching, so he emailed them off. Thirty minutes later, a grave looking school principal, Doug James, called Skye and Adrian and Jenny Grant and her mother aside to a nearby classroom and explained what he'd been told.

"Sergeant Gower has just been on the phone to me. There was an incident involving Cassandra Alvos out at 'The Gregory Blockhouse' last night. She has given a statement to the police. Fred and Marg Bleakley are taking her to Roma to stay with the parents of Andrew Thomas for a few days. She is okay physically. The Sergeant said to keep it quiet. Don't speculate or ask questions. Fred hopes to be back for the presentation tonight. He might tell you more then."

"But what happened. Was…?"

"Sorry, Adrian, that's all the Sergeant would say."

Adrian's face expressed alarm. Was it another way at getting at Streuth, the despised Greenie? Who might be next?

A query from Doug James made him refocus. "Has all the copy gone to the FC News? I know you have a report on the Consuelo Road crash but don't add anything about this incident. It will only stir up more conjecture."

Adrian knew a good reporter would be delighted to add a last-minute scoop, but grudgingly nodded consent.

"Will it be ready for distribution tonight?"

"I've just sent some more photos. The say they have ads from seven Rainworth businesses and five schools—Rocky Grammar with a half page spread. There's all our articles you have approved, including the one from Skye about pedagogy and a Q and A print interview with Uncle Barry. They say they will include some splendid bird and Nuga Nuga photos from your father's collection, Claudia, so I hope they print some of it in colour. That's what I've asked for. Delivery set for 6:30 p.m. this evening. It's a freebie!"

"Well done, Adrian. Such a great initiative."

The surprise highlight of the morning was a rehearsal of a dance presentation by eight Year 7 and Year 8 girls. Directed by Merle Gibson, all the rehearsals lacked were the costumes being prepared by Gwen Lambert and Angie Goodman whose daughters were amongst the dancers. Four girls danced to the music of the '*Dance of the Little Swans*' from the '*Swan Lake*' ballet, while Jonathan Smithson projected spectacular photos of water lily blooms and white swans at Lake Nuga Nuga. Then, two more girls to be dressed as Magpie Geese danced in to chaotic music, flapping wings and honking, honking, honking, to scatter the swans and drive them away. Finally, two girls, to be dressed as Egrets, came onto the scene to calm things down and quietly fish. Jonathan needed the girls to go through the item twice to get the lighting and timing right, and for Seb to practice the honking calls, he was mimicking as the geese caused all the disturbance. The item would follow Mandy's presentation about wildlife and the importance of retaining habitat. Misses Gibson insisted that it was needed to add some levity to the evening.

Adrian was inspecting a poster Mandy McKenzie had prepared about the rare Ooline tree species in Nuga Nuga National Park when he received confirmation the CF News was going to press. He signaled Skye with a thumbs up. The two siblings' minds turned back to the Alvos news. They both wondered who might know more about what happened with Cassie. "Could it be possible she was attacked?" Skye asked as she approached him.

"Well, there needs to be a good reason for the victim statement."

"Why her, and not me? She's the mysterious beauty, of course. I'm just a silly everyday schoolgirl."

"Sam Goodman?" Adrian suggested, ignoring the implication of Skye's remark. "Or Angie? She's here. Strange things, much more than the weather, get talked about at the Service Station. Comings and goings. Rumours." And he also thought, but didn't add, *the latest crude jokes about locals. Some things never fit for young ears*.

By midday, with the preparations for the evening winding up, Adrian had the full story of the attempted rape and the arrests. He was not sure what to share with Skye. Better it came from her mother.

Andrew's parents welcomed their visitors to their sprawling Queenslander home in Roma, just two streets away from Bradley's office. Janise had set up for a luncheon on the wide veranda, looking out over the garden full on native plants in flower.

"Have a drink first, enjoy the view of the garden and the noisy honeyeaters feeding. Our meal can wait a while."

Fred and Brad each accepted a beer in a stubby holder. The ladies opted for white wine.

"It will be lovely to have you for a few days, Connie, Janise misses having our daughter home. Paula's at ANU in Canberra, working on a doctorate in anthropology."

"I'm so very thankful that you can help me out. Just had to get away from the scene of the crime for a while."

"Of course, dear, and you'll want to see Andrew in the hospital."

"I'd love to sit and talk with him as long as he'll put up with me. Does he know about the attack?"

"A little," Janise said. "I phoned him briefly this morning. We've left the details to you."

"Fred said it was Senior Sergeant McLeod from the stock squad and his constable on the spot immediately your alarm went off. Brought one of the thugs back here to the lockup in Roma."

"They saved me from something dreadful. I would rather have died than be raped."

"I'm sure Connie doesn't want to relive that horror right now. After we've eaten, I'll settle Connie into Paula's room and perhaps you, Marg and Fred, go ahead to the hospital first with Brad."

When the others had left, Connie fell into Janise's arms. They both needed to release the pent up anger, Janise going on hugging in her compassion, thinking how awful it would have been for her own daughter; Connie accepting the comfort of another woman, a sense of being loved and safe.

Paula's bedroom also looked out across part of the veranda to the garden. "Thank you, Misses Thomas, its lovely. Such a beautiful room."

"And you have your own bathroom. The department have added an en-suite for Bradley and me. I've put towels in there for you. There's shampoo and conditioner if you wish to use it. It's just down the hall. If you don't have enough clothes while you're here, you can use some of Paula's. Size 14, much the same as you. There's plenty of space in this wardrobe for your things. I'm so glad you agreed to come here. Wonderful having another woman in the house for a while."

As Connie unpacked her few things, Janise put her head back in round the door jam. "I see you didn't bring your tennis gear. We play Tuesday nights. You'll have a choice of Paula's tennis outfits, and we have spare racquets. Her tennis shoes might fit as well. Want to see that fabled backhand Andrew has told me about."

For two hours, Connie sat beside Andrew's hospital bed. He was drowsy, falling in and out of sleep, the sedatives having their effect. While he was awake, she talked. Telling of the fear that gripped her during the attack, that horrible man pushing his repulsive bearded face at her, yelling orders at his accomplishes, the police flash light lighting up his privates—now, in hindsight, so funny she could scream with delight. Then, the distraught Bleakleys there to help. Not knowing what to say.

Andrew listened, said sorry, and squeezed her hand often. They both wanted comfort. Both wanted explanations. What had happened, that was evident. What it meant, what was the reasoning of their attackers, brains muddied by ignorant perceptions and racist-type thinking. Eight months earlier, she had attacked herself. Thrown herself into the Fitzroy, an act intended to put an end to her misery, the abhorrent fear of revelation. The torment in her mind shut off forever.

While he slept, she examined the room. There were four beds in the ward, two others occupied, their fragile privacy provided by a curtain screen. It was all so sterile, everything virgin white, a T.V. high above, suspended from the ceiling. The only colour, a vase of flowers and a green landline phone on the bedside table. The telephone was not there when she sat in the same place on Friday. It surely was arranged by his mother—not prepared to rely on Andrew's mobile being charged and switched on.

Whose voice had Andrew listened to with incoming calls? His mother's, Janise, and perhaps his father. Fred and Marg, though they hadn't said so. His principal, Mister James? Penny Mattingley, perhaps, and even the seductive Skye piling on the charm. What would Skye say, what would she be thinking? Would she be bold enough to imagine him taking her to bed? Would she wonder about how it would feel? Would she be as nervous as I would be? Would she think of blowjobs or his tongue exciting her clitoris—after all, she was a modern teenager with access to porn. One can't bear believing it possible, but I do, and the more thought I give it, the more I want it to be me. Me in his arms, me in his bed. Me losing my virginity.

Both Alana and I had been attacked on the streets of Rockhampton. Perhaps, it had to do with our Spanish beauty. The allure of the exotic. Maybe just opportunistic assaults. Alana was experienced, quick to react, not averse to being violent in response. I suffered more. I had more to protect. Alana had known several men. She was choosy, careful, but prepared to take a relationship to the level of consensual sex. She hadn't stumbled like me, withdrawn, refused. There was a surfie boy in Spain, handsome and fun-loving, his desires so transparent. I turned him away, not because I didn't like him enough but because the terror of being handled down there again, of being penetrated.

Andrew, are you listening?

He came around again when a young nurse came in with his medication and a glass of juice. She offered Connie tea but she declined.

"You may stay a while longer, if you like," the nurse said.

"Thank you, but I should go shortly."

"There's no visiting tonight, it's Saturday. No night visiting in the weekends, so stay on while you can." There was an informed wink from the nurse as she left. "I'll see he has a comfortable night."

"She's Lizzy, half Asian as you can tell, Taiwanese mother."

"So you're already flirting with all the nurses."

"Wasted chance otherwise. Now give me a kiss."

Connie responded with a peck on his cheek.

"Are you that direct with all of the female nurses, asking for kisses?"

"Definitely not. No different from all my students."

"Tell me. What about Skye. Has she phoned you?"

"Yes, Friday afternoon, now that you ask. She was concerned. Poor thing, she wanted help with an article for the CF News special edition. You've heard about that."

"Yes, Fred was explaining it on the drive here to Roma."

"Adrian, her brother, who was behind it all, bullying her to write an article about the real purpose of the dam proposal project. So I explained the pedagogy behind it."

"And was she satisfied?"

"Only when I agreed to write some brief notes for her on my iPhone and send it back within half an hour. So that had to end the call."

"No endearments?"

"Whatever you or others may think, Skye's still a dizzy school girl. Romantic in an immature way. She's not a rival for you."

"I'm impressed. Such a mature man."

Then, she kissed him, this time full on the lips. "See you tomorrow. No doubt Skye will be here. You can look forward to all the news about tonight's grand presentation."

Fred Bleakley phoned from the Rainworth School at 7:00 p.m., telling Andrew the newspaper had arrived. "The Grade 10 boys not in your geography class are doing a good job as ushers and making sure each family get a copy of the newspaper. The paper has an editorial about the student revolt when the field trip was cancelled and how it led to the presentation night. It quoted the principal, Mister James, and his praise for the students as well all those who rallied behind them. I can see that Adrian's front page report on your crash is raising eyebrows, the revelations about foul play. And Skye's article about your teaching approach is excellent, though perhaps over the heads of a lot of the readers, even to some extent, me."

"Are the celebrities there, the regional director included?"

"Yes, Skye and Mister James are escorting Ms. Sutcliffe and the mayor from Emerald around all the displays. I see Skye is introducing each student in turn, as they stand by and comment on their displays. And Jenny Grant is doing the same with Les Smallbone and Councillor Stevens. The crowd is swelling, there's quiet background music and a welcome on the big screen. No need for panic. Everything is going well. You'll get a full report tomorrow."

Chapter 15

Sunday, 18 September 2016

It was the Skye show. The nursing staff had helped Andrew into a wheelchair and pushed him out into the garden courtyard so all his visitors could gather around.

"You should have been there, Sir, it was so, so, so exhilarating! Guy was the best. His Power Point slides were really clever—showing a dam wall at Warrinilla going up layer by layer, a big storm filling the lake and the existing Lake Nuga Nuga going under, 'Just like what happened to beautiful Lake Peddar in Tasmania is 1972'. Jonathan Smithson projected the before and after photos from a Tasmanian history site. Guy then mimed swimming and fishing in a bigger Lake Warrinilla and then struck a pose of disappointment with the water draining away. Seb started whistling the call of a Whistling Kite, as Jonathan projected a series of beautiful photos of Nuga Nuga, as it is now including one of yours, Consuela, of children feeding ducks and swans on the water's edge."

"Go on, Skye, what else?' Janise called.

"The bird dance following Mandy's wildlife presentation was so much fun. Everyone was cackling with laughter when the magpie geese broke up the swan's dance, and then the egrets came in to restore peace and hustle the geese away. All done to music. The clapping went on and on after that. The girls all took several bows, and brought Misses Gibson out as well. The dance item was her idea."

Penny spoke up, aware of Skye's deliberate omission. "Jenny Grant did the difficult job of presenting the economic pros and cons of a new dam, explaining that increased irrigation could see farm chemicals infiltrate the ground water and contaminate our bore water. Everyone was alarmed at the thought."

Marg Bleakley quickly countered. "We were so proud of you, Skye, your own opening and closing pieces and how you compered the whole event."

"They all did very well." Gareth added. "It turned out a wonderful night. The last item was something special, the song by Sonny Thornton with the backing of the girls' choir."

"What did he sing?" Connie asked. She had been busy with her camera.

"The Neil Young song, *'Mother Earth'*, and he changed the last verse, when called back on stage." Adrian said.

Skye made a flourish to hand Andrew a copy of the words knowing he had a good singing voice. They sang together:

"Oh, Comet land
Can you let this go
(Down by the stream
Where the cotton grows
Respect Mother Earth
And her giving ways

Or trade away
Our children's days
Or trade away
Our child—ren's days.)"

Andrew dismissed the clapping and quickly asked, looking towards Fred Bleakley, "How did the regional director respond to all of it?"

"I heard her telling Simon Stevens, the Councillor, how she was blown away with the use of technology and the quality of the Power Point slides. She asked him about Guy, did he know the boy. 'He's my nephew,' Simon had replied proudly. "When I see him, he only talks about becoming a helicopter pilot, that's his ambition. I now see he has other talents he could use on the stage."

"And Les Smallbone?"

"I believe he grudgingly admitted to Angie Goodman how he was greatly impressed."

"We haven't congratulated Adrian on the newspaper," Marg shouted out over the ensuing conversation.

"A wonderful initiative, Adrian," Bradley Thomas used his big voice and pushed Adrian forward. "An excellent lead story on Andrew's crash. I'm sure you all agree we hope Josh Gibson gets appropriate recognition for saving Andrew's life."

"Also, we trust the courts will not be lenient with whoever drove the mine truck and with Connie's violent attackers." Janise added.

"I'm going to open some champagne and Janise has brought some cake."

Brad popped open the bottle and poured the champagne into paper cups while Janise cut the cake and Penny handed it around.

"Here's to Andrew, Connie, Adrian, and especially, the lovely Skye, who needs her parents' permission to taste this drop."

"My daughter, amazes me," Gareth said, offering her a sip from his cup. "Now, go back over and receive Andrew's praise, while we all close our ears."

Andrew put down his wine cup and took her hand. He needed to say he loved her, how wonderful she was, but feared, as always, his intent would be misconstrued. That she would reply with equal affection and with much more passion in her voice. "I haven't read your article yet. I will look forward to how brilliant it is, as Fred Bleakley told me on the phone last night."

"I just repeated your words, really. Just strung them together into sentences."

"We've entered a new world, Skye, and indeed the sky is the limit for you if you apply yourself."

"I've decided to study law when I leave school. I suppose it's Rocky Grammar next year and then Uni. I believe UQ is the best. I want to specialise in environmental law. Fight cases to protect the natural world that you so love."

"It's early in your life to make that decision."

"How old were you when you committed yourself to being a teacher. You know, the 'When I grow up I want to be…'"

"A butcher, a baker, a candlestick maker."

"No, seriously?"

“I was just 15, going on 16, like you. Determined I could do better than the teachers at Roma High.”

“So there, I’m not being silly, believing I can do it.”

“Well, all I can say to that is Australia needs your talent. I’ll follow your career closely.”

She whispered in his ear. “I know I have to give way to Connie. I can tell she needs you, but I’ll always remember how I’ve loved you, Sir.”

“Please understand you were never in the race, if that’s what you mean.”

“I know. I’m but a teary-eyed teenage dreamer, 12 years too young.”

She bent forward and they exchanged little kisses. Skye, bold enough to kiss him lightly on the lips and Andrew, in return, on the side of her face, as he eased her gently away.

Tuesday, 20 September 2016

It was midmorning when Consuela arrived at the Roma hospital in good spirits. Andrew was sitting up in bed, smiling a greeting. “How are you? How’s the pain?” she asked.

“I’m coping. Apparently, I have a pinched nerve in the neck from the whiplash. The transferred pain goes to my shoulder and all down the left arm.”

“Poor thing. Will the doctors chop your arm off, so you can play tennis in the Paralympics?’

“Don’t be frivolous. You have your own pain and bruises. They won’t leave you in a hurry.”

She had brought along two photographic prints, the one she had called *‘Andrew and his Bride’*, and another of Skye with Gareth Mattingley, her father, letting her sip from his cup of champagne.

"They are both classic photos," he said. "Do you have a name for this second one?"

"You name it, you know both of them better than me."

He thought for a while. "*'The Sip'*…no, perhaps, *'First Rights'*."

"As you sang with her, you were wincing from the pain. You could have put her off, but you struggled through with the song to please and glorify her. I'm bloody jealous as you can see. I didn't know you had such a good singing voice. You haven't sung for me like you did on Sunday with the duplicitous Skye."

Andrew deliberately ignored Connie's vengefulness. He had prepared for this anticipated challenge.

"Do you know this song?" And despite the discomfort in his chest and left arm, Andrew began singing. "I'll know when my love comes along…"

"Guys and Dolls," she butted in, and responded by singing the words to him in Spanish. *"Yo sabré..."*

When Andrew had sung all the verses and the chorus twice, Connie asked, "How come you know it so well? Or have you been listening to a YouTube clip on your smartphone, then rehearsing, so you could sing it to tease me?"

"I sang it in the lead role in a school musical, here at Roma High."

"Really?"

"It's true. I'm not faking it. Making up a story." There was a little disappointment in her eyes so he added. "But yes, I like the idea that you feel it as a tease. Does it fit? Have I stung you?"

"Streuth! You're a nasty B, Andrew Thomas," and she motioned to slap him on the left shoulder.

"Careful," he called, thrusting out his right arm to defend himself. "This body's in a delicate state."

Connie apologised, somewhat amused and delighted, rather than continuing with a show of anger.

"Who else have you sung those words to in your '*calm steady voice*'?"

"Maybe a dozen or so, I haven't kept count."

"Does that include Skye?"

"Even if I had the chance, she doesn't have the right… '*Chemistry*'. And trust me, I've said it before, I believe, that I have the '*strong moral fibre*' to resist her schoolgirl charms."

"She has a good singing voice and '*wisdom in her head*'."

"She's attractive and clever, but she doesn't make me '*stop and stare*'." And he sang again in little more than a whisper, "I'll know long before we can speak…"

Consuela put her head on his lap and listened. The lyrics were right, they didn't need to speak.

Andrew was stroking Connie's hair, imagining the pleasure of sharing a queen bed with her when a male nurse walked in and interrupted their quiet intimacy.

"Excuse me, Miss, I have to put Andrew in a wheel chair and take him for a shower. Can you wait outside, or go for a walk. Perhaps, about 30 minutes?"

In the afternoon, they chatted about his students, the ones who had phoned since the Saturday night triumph.

"Guy's uncle has arranged for him to go flying with the helicopter pilot, a fellow who's helping with the muster of the Planet Downs hill blocks. Guy will be in raptures. Flying choppers is his ambition. It was partly the reason for him to study geography—understand landscape, climate, weather patterns, storms and turbulence."

"And the aboriginal boy, Seb?"

Angie Goodman told me Seb is happy working for his father in the garage throughout the holidays. He can be apprenticed next year."

"And the girls?"

"Jane is off to Maryborough for the school aged equestrian competition, expecting to win a few ribbons; and Danielle, our young jockey, just 16 this week, has been given the mount on her dad's top filly in a horse race this Saturday here in Roma."

"So the phone's running hot. And I suppose they all say, *'I wish you could be there to see me, Sir.'*"

"I can't help my popularity. And while I think of it, talk about a star—Mandy Macpherson is off to the Writers Festival in Brisbane. Her mother says she has written and illustrated a children's story about a platypus who is envious of the birds and leaves his pond to grow wings."

"And does this platypus learn to fly?"

"I asked the same question, and Mandy squealed into the phone, *'Yes, he does, but he can't sing! When he tries, with his hard pallet and broad flat bill, the sound comes out like a honking noise. Honk, Honk. He becomes a Magpie Goose.'*"

"Imaginative. I suppose you claim some credit because you taught Mandy English as well as geography?"

“Yes I did, in Grade 9. But her creativity is all her own. She already has lined up a meeting with a children’s story publisher while in Brisbane.”

“Well, I know both Jenny and Grace may also be very fond of you, but I suspect they really hate me.”

“Why do you say that?”

“Claudia told me her whole family were going to camp for two weeks on North Keppel Island and take Grace with them as company for Jenny. Because of the rape attack and me recovering here in Roma, she is stuck working at the bank till I get back to Rainworth Downs. The girls wouldn’t go without Claudia, so they are at home being sour with everybody.”

“Pity for Grace. She will be putting in the daylight hours at her parents’ news agency and waitressing at her uncle’s Chinese restaurant at night.”

“And I believe Jenny is employed by the uncle as well on busy nights. I should really be back there, so Claudia can take her leave and go with the girls to join her husband, Don, and the boys. Mister Smithson can’t employ Jonathan at the bank to replace me. He wouldn’t even consider it.”

“You know Smithson phoned yesterday evening and thanked me for encouraging Jonathan to take his mind off computer games for the month or so of the project. He said Jonathan can now see a future opening up for him in IT.”

“And what of the partially blind girl?”

“Josie? She is so conscientious in all she does. She’s a battler. I suspect she will go out to the Sapphire gem fields during the holiday to help her parents at their prospecting claim. Let’s hope they have some luck. She needs it.”

“You know what this has been leading us back to?”

"Skye?"

"Yes, the oh-so-charming Miss Mattingley, calling you every day, for a loving chat."

"Don't get so alarmed or bitter. Penny forced her to text me an apology about the 'kiss'. It read, *'Sorry about my unethical behaviour. Forgive me'*."

"I'm sure you thought there was nothing to forgive. You can't deny you enjoyed that little kiss. I filmed it on my camera. The smiling acceptance."

"She's a kid. Like kissing a favourite uncle."

"And you're an adult, not a relative, but a teacher, pledged to set an example. You have been far too cosy with that…"

"You've been listening to my mother. I got the same lecture yesterday."

"And next, you'll get it from your father. And I'm surprised you haven't had it before this from your school principal."

"Can't we drop this? Penny told me that the four Mattingleys were leaving today for ten days on the Gold Coast. Skye's forbidden to phone me. Most likely, she'll have met some handsome surfer and forgotten about me by the time they return to Rainworth."

"Just ten days, hardly likely, no matter how good she looks in a bikini. If she can't surf, she'd have to pass the sex willingness test to entice attention."

"Now, you're being unjustly crude."

"Don't forget, I belonged to the surf culture in Spain for almost four years. I was nobody till I could catch and ride a big wave."

"And did you pass the sex test as well as the surfing test?"

"I had a regular boyfriend for a year. Paulo was incredibly handsome and charming. He and I, with my male cousins, tripped to surfing beaches all around Spain and Portugal. Even a trip to Tenerife out in the Atlantic. Wonderful beaches and surf in the Canary Islands. Paulo's attentiveness kept others away. There was a moral code amongst the surfers, when a chick was bespoken, the other guys backed off."

"So it didn't last—you and Paulo?"

"Paulo became tired of my rejections when it came to sex. I wouldn't let him touch me down there. I froze every time he tried. I knew why but couldn't explain to him. I hated myself for it."

She took hold of his right hand. He felt the shudder going through her body.

"I went close to giving myself to him several times. I wanted to please him. He would get frantic, desperate, but I wasn't brave enough to go through with it. My brain telling me it was debasing, unclean, crude."

Andrew wasn't sure what to say. Where he really stood in regard to their relationship.

"Well, do I have a chance? Will your vulva, your vagina, also always remain off limits to me?"

He could have bit his tongue as the words tumbled out, but she smiled and squeezed his hand tightly, appreciating his frankness, that signal that her attractiveness to him was also sexual. It meant she would have to deal with it. Deal with letting him explore.

After a long pause, she responded, "I can't say. Let's just be close friends for now." The quivering in her body giving a different message.

He saw the emotional anger in her face. Anger at herself. Anger about things in her past. Something had been welling up in him ever since her visit the previous Friday. The rape attack just made the feelings more uncontrolled in him. The need to declare himself while being a part of her healing.

"I'm bedridden in Roma for another four or five weeks, and you'll be back at work in Rainworth Downs. I want you to know I'll find that unbearable. Even just one day, Connie, without looking into your eyes, will be torture for me. The pain in my pelvis and chest is nothing in comparison."

Connie's left hand went to cover her mouth, the breath that was caught there would have to be released in a gasp. When it came, she couldn't control the explosion—the moans and sighs, and the tears she fought to hold back.

"There! I've said it," Andrew went on. "Not that *'I'll know'*, but *'I'm sure'*, and I hope you are too."

It was too much. His love for her undeserved. His physical desires would cause a calamity if she allowed this to progress. So she attacked.

"A brave declaration. Are you sure it's not just a single man's fantasy rather than true love? Unfortunately, you have no surfing credentials. And if you do have experience, can you handle the wave break that is coming? It will be your test."

Andrew fell silent. He'd been rebuffed. Ridiculed even in a kindly way. How he wished to know but daren't ask what Connie was implying with her riddles.

Wednesday, 21 September 2016

Doctor David Wu was with Andrew when his morning visitors arrived. Andrew introduced them as, “My mother, Janise, and a good friend, Consuela.”

“Andrew is progressing well. From tomorrow, the physiotherapist will start him doing chair exercises, and some short walks with an upright rollator. If all goes well, this man will be walking by himself in two weeks. No rollator or crutches, just a single walking stick.”

“How soon till he might be discharged?”

“Hard to say, maybe three weeks. He has some neck problems; we are also working on. X-rays show there’s some damage to the third and fourth vertebrae that could continue to cause problems for him in the future, but everything else will heal naturally.”

“You’re a lucky fellow, Andrew, the damage to your body from such a crash could have been a great deal worse. And you have two lovely women to go on caring for you.”

Andrew listened while Janise was full of talk about the tennis. How well Connie played. How Brad and Connie had won a mixed doubles against the best pairing in the social group. How she’d been invited back on to make up the numbers in a men’s set. The backhand and the winning lobs.

“It was fun,” Connie said. “I really enjoyed it.”

“Connie looked lovely in Paula’s favourite white top and pale green skirt.”

“And it was good that Paula’s tennis shoes fitted.”

The talk turned to it being St. Matthew’s Day and the hope there would be no repeat of the 1998 incident in Rainworth Downs. Fred Bleakley had phoned to say Sergeant Gower was making sure there was a strong police presence in the town just in case. Les Smallbone said he'd walk the streets defiantly, but in reality after Saturday night, all the unrest had settled down.

"Fred claimed that the egrets had flown in with a white peace banner." Connie added with a laugh.

Then, Janise announced Andrew's grandfather, the Lieutenant-Colonel Gus Thomas, was expected to be in town in the afternoon to visit Andrew in hospital and then meet up at with family and friends for dinner at the RSL Club.

"Brad and I want him to meet Consuela. He'll no doubt fall in love with her and propose on the spot, the old rascal."

"I've never been wooed by a Lieutenant-Colonel. That will be a hoot. I presume he's no longer in the army?"

"He's 75 and well and truly retired. Lives with his third wife in Toowoomba." Andrew explained. "Worked his way up through the ranks. Two postings with the infantry in Vietnam and saw combat in skirmishes in Bouganville and the Solomons while on peace keeping missions."

"He's like royalty at the RSL here in Roma, Janise added. "You'll see tonight. He'll definitely charm you, like he does all the women. His first wife, Brad's mother, died from breast cancer when Gus was in Vietnam the first time. That hit him really hard. I had only just met Brad then, and I could see how badly everyone in his family and the whole town here were grieving. His second wife had been a smoker. She was a real bundle of fun, but unfortunately, suffered a heart attack at age 62. His third wife is Asian, Vietnamese, 20 years Gus's junior. Came to Australia as a child refugee. Very attentive and loving. The marriage seems to work for both of them."

Janise went to get herself some coffee, leaving Andrew and Connie to talk privately.

"After the first stumbling blocks, you continue to impress my mother. Tennis included."

"I hope it's justified. Like you, she hardly knows me. The inner me. Not just the superficial."

"But I am thankful, I learn more every day you are here. When are you returning to Rainworth?"

"Your dad's taking me back to the Bleakley's tomorrow. He said he is going on to Salvator Rosa in the Carnarvon National Park to inspect some improvements recently made to the camp site."

"Salvator Rosa, the most scenic part of the whole park. Major Mitchell, the explorer, wrote glowingly about it. His party had travelled north through the dry Warrego country where there were only scattered waterholes. When crossing the range, they came upon a deep running creek—spring fed with beautifully clear water, full of life and nourishment and a spectacular backdrop of what he called *'ruined castles and forts'*. He named the area Salvator Rosa after an Italian landscape artist whose work he admired."

"And you obviously love it in the same way. Such passion, and the desire to teach about it, may not leave much time for a woman and family in your life."

"Life's an unfolding landscape, don't you think? There will be joys and disappointments. If the weather is bad, you must still find your way."

"But it can become so bleak that you really want to end it, and you now know I tried. I can't rule out more frightening weather ahead for either of us. I can't say I could ever commit to a permanent relationship, to marriage."

Chapter 16

Sunday, 16 October 2016

Andrew and Consuela were alone. They sat side by side at a table in the picnic area above Virgin Rock.

Andrew had been discharged from Roma Base Hospital on the previous Monday, 10 October. His best mate and father had picked him up in a green Suzuki Jimny which looked brand new to Andrew, it being in such good condition.

Andrew explained as they were driving the winding road up into Minerva Hills, "It has been a Queensland Government vehicle assigned to the Police Stock Squad and replaced after three years by a 2016 model. It was to come up for a government auction, but my dad was able to jump in and make a good offer a little above estimated market value. So now, it's mine. 'Pay me off when you can,' my dad said, There's no hurry. After the court case, you should get an insurance and third-party payout for the old Jimny, so that'll help.'"

"What court case?"

"Two mine employees have been charged with stealing a vehicle and reckless driving causing an accident. Sergeant Gower wanted to make it a charge of attempted murder, but his superiors didn't think the evidence was strong enough to make that stick. There was the matter of the distraction of a phone call just before the accident. The defence could make a lot out of that, when it goes to court."

"What phone call?"

"My mobile rang just before the truck hit. I didn't answer. I pulled over simply to avoid the rampaging truck."

"Do you know who it was trying to contact you?"

It was a mistake, to mention the call, and now he dreaded the confession.

"Yes, I checked the voice mail when I received my phone back."

"And?"

"It was Skye."

"The little vixen. She's was abusing your trust."

"Please, Connie, don't go there again. She was concerned, having heard I'd been called to the police station the night before. Nothing more than that."

The shame and annoyance showed as he hit the accelerator on a steep pinch, and the Suzy responded, shedding gravel and dust behind them. They landed awkwardly on the uphill side of a steep bump, Connie holding tight to the side strap while pushing against the dashboard.

She thought a lot about Andrew's petulance but didn't comment. "Did they find the mine truck?"

"Yes. In Serecold State Forest, as my dad suspected. Josh Gibson and a mate from Rewan Station came across it, rammed into a huge gum tree—no doubt trying to disguise the fact that the driver had been involved with an earlier accident. The two who have been charged claim that they had been put up to it by that bugger they call Bluebeard, Cormac O'Brien, who led the rape attempt on you."

"Fred told me O'Brien has been before a magistrate in Rockhampton, and that trial is set for early 2017. Unlike his mates, O'Brien's being kept in custody till the trial date."

"I apologise, my bad driving. My dad insisted it wasn't legal for me to drive Suzy's Mark 2 till I got a clearance from a GP in town there in Roma. Since I was walking quite well with a stick and my pelvis and ribs pretty well healed, it was a formality, except for my mobility in my neck which is still bothering me. So anyway, I stayed on with my mother and father for a few days while that driver's permit was sorted out. It was good to have some time with my parents and hear their feelings about you and about your night out in Roma at the RSL, but my heart was here, Connie, to be in close contact with you."

"Your grandfather and father were so chivalrous that night. So now I have three generations of Thomas men who crave my attention, Gus, Bradley, and yours truly. Which one should I choose?"

"We all know a good dish when we meet one. I'd hope you go for youth before charm. Actually, my great-grandfather was also a ladies man. An early free settler in the Roma district, he had children to three different women and didn't marry any of them. Quite a rogue. Grandma, Gus's mother, was a Bidjara woman, so I have a smidgen of aboriginal blood."

"My mother can tell you similar stories about our Spanish family. Rogue romantics are not confined to the Australian bush."

"Family history aside, can you now tell me why you so wanted me to bring you here?"

"Let us first have the picnic lunch Marg prepared for us and then…we'll see."

While they ate, they joked about Marg, her choice of picnic food, the sandwich fillings, the lady finger bananas, and the home-baked apple tart.

After they had finished and had drunk their ginger beer, Consuela walked over to the lookout rail, the countryside spread out before her. It seemed at that moment so jumbled and chaotic like the story of her life, with the sanctuary of a loving home perhaps only to be found in the far distance. A sudden anxiousness spread through her gut. Should she jump? Part of the stress inside her body dared her to scale the fence and leap. She had done it before on the Fitzroy River bridge, yet a quiet voice in her head said "No!" …was it her mother or Uncle Climent, she wasn't sure. She took an enormous deep breath and turned back to see Andrew hobbling towards her.

"I must struggle through the revelation—my virgin story. I owe it to you. A chance for you to catch a thunderous wave and ride it with me. It's not going to be easy, and if we both arrive safely on the shore, you must promise to be gentle with me."

"May I first ask this question? Is something to do with junior tennis?"

Connie nodded, turning away again and holding back her misery—the fear of confessional block. With her back to him, she replied. "No questions or I'll shut like a clam. There will be no relief in it for either of us. I have to tell it my way.

"I was 12, about to turn 13 when I won both the Queensland Primary School Championship and the State under 14 championship. The State Junior Coach, Gavin Davis, was at both tournaments and approached my mother to have me join his junior squad for 15–18-year-olds."

Andrew went to speak, to say he had been in the State junior squad before Davis took over, but Connie silenced him, pointing at him with intent, then holding the pointing finger across her lips.

"So I was signed up and attended a number of coaching sessions in Rockhampton, where Gavin Davis got me to play more aggressively, like a boy, he said, and persuaded me to have my hair cut short and wear a cap backwards, like Lleyton Hewitt, as a reminder to be tenacious. It worked, and I kept winning tournaments in Mackay, Townsville, and then Brisbane. My mother was impressed with the results, and I was starting to think big—Australian Open, Wimbledon, and all that. *'Spanish-Australian star takes on the world.'* I was full of myself. I was practicing all the time and doing daily gym sessions. My schoolwork at the historic Range Convent was neglected most of the time. I couldn't care less about study or school results.

"Then, Gavin Davis talked my mother into letting me go to a junior squad camp at Gympie. It was a five-day camp for 15–18 year old girls, senior secondary school kids, but he told her I was good enough to beat most of the girls who would be there, and I deserved to be part of it. I'd never travelled to a tournament without my mother and often Alana as well, so I was nervous about it, but I decided I should go. Mum paid the bill and waved me goodbye on the train to Gympie with a 17-year Rocky Grammar girl, Glenda Edwards, whom I hardly knew.

"On the second day of the camp, I developed a thigh strain, and that night, Gavin Davis, 'Coach', we all called him at camp. He came to the room I shared with Glenda in the campsite accommodation wing. He offered to massage my thigh, and wanting to be fit for the next day, I agreed. He used some massage oil and then Voltaren gel, and it seemed like it was doing a lot of good. After he left, Glenda said something like, 'be careful with Coach, he's a bit of a grub. Gets in your knickers given half a chance,' but I just thought she was jealous of me and ignored it."

She could see Andrew was desperate to speak, "I knew Gl—" but Connie went quickly on.

"On the third afternoon, Glenda was horribly sick and rushed off to Gympie hospital with suspected appendicitis. The female assistant coach went with her and stayed that night at the hospital. Coach came to my room again, asking about my left thigh, and I told him I had played on during the day, but it was quite sore. So he asked me to strip my pj pants off, and he did the massage again. This time, he could work right up to the top of my leg while I lay on my tummy and explained how the muscle was tight right up close to my bum. It didn't occur to me that his attention was indecent or that he was grooming me for something more sinister. When he got me to roll back over, he rubbed the gel right up to touch my panties. Coach made some remark when I twitched, that it was a sign my body knew the massage was doing a lot good. I'd had my first period the year before and had become used to accommodating my monthly discharge, but it wasn't my time of month and couldn't understand the horrified feeling induced by that touch to my panties."

"You should have known then it was abuse and reported him."

"Please, Andrew, let me go on. I know now I was naive. Anyway, Coach stopped and left, and I was pleased the next day that quad muscle was again fine for most of the day. I played the top senior player and it was four all when Coach called the match off, so I was feeling really great. That night after dinner, the female coach went off to see Glenda at the hospital where she had her appendix out during the day. I was again alone in my room and wondered if Coach would come and massage my sore quad muscle again because it was important to me to be able to play again the next day. When he came in, he closed the door and asked me would I like another massage. I sheepishly agreed, but I had not changed into my pj's and defied his request to strip by keeping my playing shorts on. Nevertheless, I just lay down on my back with legs slightly apart, and he started on my left leg, then moved his hands to the right as well, so I was more open to him. He took out this thing he said was a vibrator and that it could do the muscles more good than his hands. He switched it on and rubbed it up and down both legs, the tingling exciting me."

Connie stopped for a moment. Andrew's expression assured her he was surfing a big wave with her. There was fear and dread in his eyes.

"Then, Coach pushed the tip of the dildo past my shorts and rubbed it over my undies, so the vibrations excited my vulva lips. I knew it was not right but strangely, like first catching a big wave, I felt I wanted that thrill to continue.

When Coach pushed the vibrator inside me past the protection of my knickers. I could feel the wetness in my vagina ooze out and moisten my labia. I was conflicted—trapped in the barrel of the wave, knowing it was a terrible choice but also in fear of Coach. He had the physical strength and the power which appeared to leave me helpless. When, with another thrust, the vibrator broke through my hymen, that trance I was in was broken by the pain. The wave was crashing down around me, and I yelled 'Get out! You Mongrel!' yanking his hand away, pushing the dildo into his face.

"'Sorry,' he said as if it was unintentional, that he had done nothing wrong. He stood up, took the vibrator and other paraphernalia and left me flabbergasted and humiliated…mumbling countless expletives before crying myself to sleep."

There was nothing to do but stretch their hands across the table between them and hold on tight while their heads touched for comfort.

After a long pause, Connie coughed repeatedly, as if needing to dispel a bucket full of salty ocean water from her chest. Andrew squeezed tight till she calmed herself.

"So Andrew…that's how it was. A brief buoyant thrill followed by the wipeout."

"I'm here on the beach with you, Connie. That despicable bastard of a tennis coach is nowhere to be seen. We're both safe!" And he moved around the table to sit beside her, cuddling her shaking body, and gently kissing her on the head and forehead multiple times.

"On the final day, I pleaded I had started my period and refused to go back on the court. Gavin Davis was furious with me, but not as furious as I was with him! I thought the female coach might at least come and comfort me, but it didn't happen. I just clammed up and spoke to no one."

Tears and kisses over, Andrew suggested they take a walk—any admission that he needed regular short walks to re-strengthen the weakened muscles was anathema to him. His role for Consuela was to be both physically and mentally strong. Not to admit to weakness.

They set off, holding hands, Andrew grudgingly using a walking stick. Connie remained silent while Andrew talked about the geology and vegetation pointing at features with his stick—the acid volcanic rocks, the thin soils, the struggling mallee eucalypts, the native shrubs in flower, the basket ferns, and the felt orchids in little crevices. "There's beauty in every landscape," he said, "if you know where to look for it."

They had gone about a kilometre along the rough trail when they stopped at a bench seat and sat for a rest. Connie put her arm around Andrew, careful not to squeeze, knowing he still had some soreness from the broken ribs. "Thanks, Andrew," Connie murmured, "you're a treasure." And then, when he grinned back at her, she continued in a clearer voice, "I'd been waiting so long, it seems, to have the courage to open up to you. I'm relieved you now know. It was nearly ten years ago, but I still remember as if it was only yesterday, the worst day of my life. I took refuge for almost five years with family in Spain. I was 19 when I returned. It was just before all the publicity started in Australia about institutional child abuse—the Royal Commission into Sexual Child Abuse. I tried to ignore the revelations about the clergy and schools till one child's evidence that was widely publicised triggered my horrid memories of the tennis camp incident. The fear of revelation frightened me. Not even my family had been told the truth. I gradually went back into depression until it became severe. I wanted to 'come out' yet I couldn't shake off the feeling of the victim's guilt. It all became so debilitating, I tried to end it all."

She paused for a while, needing to be convinced Andrew was listening, indeed absorbed. "After the suicide attempt, when I confessed to Uncle Climent with mother and Alana present, they insisted I write a statement about my case of historical sexual child abuse, as it is called. That went to the Rockhampton police, and it has started an investigation by the Sexual Assault Investigation Unit into the dealings of Gavin Davis over the years with girls in his squad, and also the possible failure of Queensland Tennis to respond to any complaints made by girls or parents."

"And you came to Rainworth Downs to keep out of the way while the investigations went on?"

"It was Lorae's, mum's, idea. Away from the nosy press."

"I'm thinking it was meant to be, stars aligning."

"Fortuitous, yes, since we've clicked. We really enjoy each other's company. Still, that is not going to be enough for me. Lasting love needs more than attraction. There's a lot of deep bonding to do to seal a partnership. Alana has never found that. And Lorae will say she committed too early as a 22-year-old."

"Did *'I'll know'* mean nothing, when you sang it?"

"It did, yet it was a cry of hope, not conviction."

Andrew was taken aback. Romantic notions shattered by her words. He turned away, took up his walking stick, and thrust it in the air. "You keep putting up hurdles. There is a limit."

"I bring baggage with me, Andrew. I know I'll be slow with sexual intimacy. You're likely to hate that. And you're in love with your teaching. As a partner or wife, I fear I'd firstly be directed to my roles and, after that, treated as a convenience. There for sex when I offered it, and the housekeeping, while you'd spend most of your home time planning lessons and excursions or marking assignments. Not being equal in the relationship. I couldn't live like that."

"Believe me, I really want it to work as much as you. I hope you understand that, and give me a chance."

"Yes," she said quietly hushing him. "I know that feeling."

They were silent as they walked back to the car. Each considering the clash between emotion and reason.

Over dinner, at the Bleakleys, Fred asked politely, "When do you return to the school?"

"I have sick leave till the end of the month. Starting on the first day of November."

"Your students will be keen to have you back," Marg added, "Have you heard from any of them? From Skye or Guy?"

"Yes, I've been keeping in touch with the families. I'm invited to Lambert's for dinner tomorrow evening."

"Well, you might find out about Skye being in big trouble. She's been replaced as school captain. Jane Anderson got the position. Strange choice, don't you think?"

Andrew was gob smacked. He put down his cutlery and wiped his lips with the serviette provided. There was the pressure of three sets of eyes on him. Anything he said could be incriminating. He tried, but couldn't find the appropriate words.

Fred, alert to Andrew's hesitancy, came to the rescue. "Jane's family run the biggest pastoral operation in the district. They are like aristocracy around here. She's just won the cross-country event at the Queensland Schools Equestrian Championships in the holidays. She may not be the most talented academic student, but it makes sense. Recent celebrity status is hard to overlook. Probably a sensible move by Mister James. Strategic really. Surprisingly decisive as well."

"Penny told me on the phone that Skye is devastated," Marg went on.

"Did you know, Connie? Claudia would have spoken of it. It would be all around the town."

With Andrew's query, the discomfit had shifted to Connie.

"You know what, Andrew, it was not my role to tell you! I'm just a bystander. If you have a problem with it, the dismissal, you can speak up. Protest. Boycott the school. Go on strike. Yet I would hope you don't. You don't have any idea of the circumstances. Stay out of it. Let it blow over."

"But I can't ignore it. Skye will implore me to seek justice for her. To take her side."

Connie rose, fire in her face, crimson with anger. "She may be your pet student! Your little pussy! But you're not her protector! Her knight in shining armour! Get over it,

Andrew! Quickly! Or get over me!" She stormed out to head for her bedroom.

Andrew could only apologise for both of them. He stood, thanked Marg and Fred for the lovely meal and the efforts they had made, and humbly took his leave.

Chapter 17

Monday, 17 October 2016

It was Guy who answered the Lambert's front door. "Come in, Sir, Mum's in the kitchen."

She was quick to emerge and give their visitor a hug. "Great to see how well you look. Any lingering problems?"

Before he could answer, Guy's two sisters were eager to be part of the welcome, excited to tell him about the swan and geese dance, and how Guy had helped to fly a helicopter. "Mum filmed it all on her iPad."

"We can look at that after dinner. First, a drink to welcome Mister Thomas back," Gwen interrupted. "You take a seat on the deck. Guy will get the drinks. I just need to take the rice off the stove and drain it. I hope you like curried chicken, Thai style?"

The girls chattered on, talking about the presentation night and asking about Consuela—miming to accompany their words.

"She's so beautiful. Oo-la-la. You're so lucky."

"Consuela's such a lovely name. It means lovey-dovey."

"We all know Cassandra's not her real name. Secret women's business."

"She dresses and walks like a film star."

"Have you seen her wriggle her bottom?"

They strutted around the room as if in high heels and with napkins as headscarves. Before long, they were splitting themselves with laughter. Andrew induced to join in.

"Can you speak Spanish with her?"

"*Hola, mi amor?* So romantic."

"How often have you kissed?"

"Did you…?"

"That's enough," Gwen insisted, joining them. Wine for Andrew and Gwen. Soft drinks for the children. "Calm down and sit down. Give Andrew, I mean Mister Thomas, some peace."

"We know his first name, Mum."

"It's no surprise."

Gwen ignored them. "Have you heard about Skye? The ruckus at the school. Rather upsetting."

"Yes, only last night at the Bleakleys. I haven't heard from the Mattingleys since they left for their Gold Coast holiday. What happened? What did Skye do to warrant dismissal?"

"Later this evening, after we've enjoyed the dinner and the filming, the girls want you to see, Guy can fill you in on the details."

Andrew and Guy retreated to Guy's bedroom. The walls were decorated with photographs of helicopters. Chopper's in battle, carrying out rescues at sea, crop dusting, stock mustering, flying tourists over Uluru and Carnarvon Gorge.

"I see your heart's set on flying."

"Uncle Simon has been so good to me and to my mum. I had two trips in his neighbour's, the Planet Downs helicopter, over the Comet and also the Carnarvon Gorge. That was such a great experience."

"Where next year?"

"I won't leave Mum, not yet. Travel each day to Emerald High, then after Year 12, perhaps, Uncle Simon will pay for me to go to flying school somewhere. Maybe Brisbane."

"You've changed, Guy, for the better."

"After that night of the fight at the rugby club, I've dropped the gung-ho wild boy persona. As you said to us all, we need to understand ourselves and not blame others for our plight. I know where I'm going now."

"And what about Skye? Has she lost the plot? She was full of ambition last time we spoke when she visited the hospital."

"It started on the first Tuesday of term, our first geography lesson. Mister James introduced Mister Mawson. He's a pom, doing relief, teaching in Emerald and surrounding schools. We all sat in a circle and each of us explained our contribution to the presentation night and showed display charts. Before the lesson finished, Mandy said we should finish the task and put together a booklet, covering our research and conclusions. A publication that could go in the library. Mister James agreed and suggested we take the next two lessons to put it together."

"That all seems sensible."

"It was only at the beginning of the Thursday lesson that Skye wanted to take over, saying she would be the editor and started delegating tasks. Well, Jenny immediately protested and nominated Mandy for the responsibility of editing, telling Skye directly to her face that she wasn't the Queen bee; that her beloved hive master was not there; that Mandy had the literary credentials and, if necessary, they could put it to a vote."

"Well, how did Skye react?"

"She was livid, but Mister Mawson gave her no chance to sustain an objection, immediately asking for a show of hands in favour of Mandy. Five hands went up quickly. Mandy said she couldn't vote, leaving Seb and I, plus Josie and Skye. Of course, Josie had no idea what to do, but with so many hands waving in the air, she raised hers and that was it."

"Jonathan voted for Mandy?"

"I think he was just a bit fed up with Skye's bossiness. Anyway, all the tasks were allocated, and Skye was given the environmental impact segment to write."

"That surely doesn't warrant Skye being stood down as School Captain."

"It was in the playground that Skye started at Jenny, claiming she had done all the coordination leading up to the big event, she'd written the article in the newspaper about the purpose behind the study, and therefore, it was obvious she should be the editor of the report.

"Jenny, Jane, Grace, and Danielle got stuck into her. They were spiteful, calling her your sex kitten. Making secret phone calls and running off to visit you in hospital. It got quite nasty, really tacky. Then, Grace produced a love note that had fallen out of one of Skye's book. Jenny read it out, something about *'when I next see you, you may fondle and kiss my breasts'* and then read another passage I'm not game to repeat—about where this friend’s tongue was welcome.

“Skye protested vehemently. She shouted it was a personal letter she was composing to send to some surfing dude she called Scooter, whom she’d met on the Gold Coast; but the others weren’t listening. Jenny just waving the note in the air spitefully and passing it back to Grace. That’s when Skye lost it. She screamed obscenities at them all and went for Grace, wrestling her for the note, spitting and scratching her in the face, and then pushing her to the ground. All the younger kids had gathered around, shouting *‘Fight! Fight!’* Jenny and Jane pulled Skye away, laughing as she fought them, till Misses Gibson arrived and shut them up.”

“I see. Skye could say she was provoked, but it hardly excused the assault.”

“Especially, as Grace is Chinese, and it could be seen as a racist attack.”

“How is Skye in class now?”

“She’s working with Jonathan on our current tasks. Doesn’t talk to the others. Just to Seb and me.”

“Well, looks like I’ve got some healing to do, and I’m not talking about me. I return to school on the first of November.”

Tuesday, 18 October 2016

Andrew phoned Penny Mattingley.

“I heard you are back, how are you?”

“Progressing well. Can we talk this afternoon before Skye is home?”

"You've heard?"

"Yes, Guy filled me in last night. I had dinner at the Lamberts'."

"In a way, we saw it coming. Attacking the tall poppy. But she handled it abominably. Gary and I are so ashamed about what happened. We try to ignore the town gossip, but it's hard, and much worse for Skye. Do come for afternoon tea. It will be lovely to see you and tell you about our Gold Coast holiday."

Andrew and Penny had been talking over tea for an hour when Skye arrived.

"We have a visitor," Penny said. "In the lounge, go and see."

"Sir!" She was full of smiles, dropping her school bag and stepping towards him.

He offered a quick cuddle, and she felt the turbulence in her mind falling away.

"Thanks," she said and backed away. "I guess you've heard about my disgrace?"

"Don't see it as a disgrace, but a lesson in life. You're better than that, much better, and you know it."

Skye looked crestfallen.

"Have you apologised to Grace?"

"I've written an apology to the whole school. Misses Gibson helped me with it. It's posted on the notice board at the office."

"So then, I'll be demanding a face to face apology in front of the class when I return to school, first day of November. Right?"

"I know, you'd want that. But, Sir, I was provoked."

"Skye, we have to restore the harmony. Promise me you'll do it."

She hung her head for a while, then looked up at him, and nodded.

"It will do you a lot of credit." He paused while Skye accepted the implications.

"Now, how's the classroom? Mister Mawson has you working on the world major rivers study?"

"Not the most obvious ones. He restricted our choice to the Yukon in Alaska, the Mekong in Asia, the Zambezi in Africa, the Rhone in Europe, and the Tigris-Euphrates in the Middle East. I'm working with Jonathan on the Tigris-Euphrates, delving into all the history, how so many civilisations have depended on that river system."

"Good for you to be working with Jonathan?"

"He's so smart, so clever at following up leads. We're both absorbed in what we're discovering. Even watching some on location security filming at major archaeological sites."

"That's fantastic, Skye. It would appear then that Mister Mawson is following the work plan I had prepared for this term. Has the Comet River study report been finished?"

"Yes, Mandy did well, after things settled down, getting us to work to deadlines. For the environmental segment, I had the Starlee Dam environmental report to work with plus the implications for Lake Nuga Nuga if the Warrinilla site was chosen. It was time consuming, more than difficult. Rather hard to condense it into five pages."

"So what's to happen with the report?"

"Mister James is getting it printed and bound, and copies are to go to Mister Smallbone's office, the Regional

Director of Education, and the school and town libraries. He's waiting to add a foreword from you."

Penny joined them with drinks.

"Now, what's this about a Gold Coast boyfriend?"

"Oh, then you've also heard about the love letter I suppose, from Guy?"

"Pretty *risqué*, I hear. Has your mum read it?"

"Modern teenagers," Penny said. "We were more discrete when I was Skye's age."

"And is there really a boyfriend? Does Scooter exist?"

"Yes. We met in the surf. I was wearing a blue bikini, and he noticed me. He offered to teach me to ride a surfboard. He was very cute about it. I had a few goes and got to stand up twice."

Penny added, He's a nice boy, actually studies surfing at Miami High School. Blonde, curly locks, great physique. He's phoned three times since we came home, and I'm sure there are several emails and Snapchat messages back and forth. Selfie photos as well."

"Mum, stop it! It's just a little flutter. I'm not sold on him."

Penny and Andrew exchanged suppressed giggles.

"Before I go, I need your help. Consuela and I have had a disagreement over my commitment to my students, putting my teaching ahead of her. She won't like it knowing that I'm here consoling you, Skye. *'Consoling'* that will be her word for it. It could create more friction between us."

There was a long drawn out silence—expectation of a request or a further query hung there, yet neither party was forthcoming.

Skye moved uncomfortably in her seat and then stood to leave.

"Can you speak to her? Tell her I came to see both of you, not just Skye. Tell her, Penny, if you can find a way—tell her how I feel. How obvious it is that I'm so fond of her, or something to that effect. I know that sounds mushy, but let me go on."

Skye sat down again to listen.

"I've spoken to her sister, Alana, last night on the phone. Connie has to record a filmed interview with the Historical Sexual Abuse Investigation Unit on Thursday next week. Lorae and Alana both hope I'll take her down to Rockhampton, where the police have lined up some other young women as well to testify about the behaviour of the state tennis coach ten years ago. His name is Gavin Davis, and it's likely he will be charged later this year. Lorae has invited me to stay a few days with them. I desperately want Connie to agree, and let me take her to Rocky in my new Suzuki."

"What if Gareth and I invite you both to a barbecue here. This coming Sunday, midday. The Goodmans and Lamberts as well. Celebrate your return to good health. Surely, she won't refuse."

"Thanks Penny, that's a lovely idea. Connie's recovery as well."

"Fine, Skye and Adrian can help."

"I'll be unable to play tennis for a while. Has Connie been back on the court?"

"Not yet, but I'll ask her that as well. Insist we need her to make up the numbers."

Chapter 18

Sunday, 23 October 2016

Consuela was uncertain about attending the barbecue. Her mind was on the pending appearance before the Historical Sexual Abuse Unit. She needed all the sympathetic support she could muster. There was family, Lorae and Alana, and some of the girls who helped at Lorae's dance school. Claudia and the Bleakleys would offer support and there were well wishes by email from Spain. Little else. She knew she wanted Andrew to be present nearby when she testified, as if he was in the hearing with her holding her hand, yet they were hardly on speaking terms. He may not even know about the tribunal filming in Rockhampton. Still, she decided the invitation to the Mattingleys had been accepted by Marg on her behalf, and there was an obligation to front up, so she dressed smartly in the belief it would impress Andrew, and they would get together to talk.

Marg and Fred drove Consuela to the barbecue at the Mattingleys. Before they left, Marg had persuaded Connie to change into something more casual—jeans, a blue top, floral headscarf, sunglasses, a compact, hairbrush, and tissues in a handbag. No mascara or makeup, pale lipstick, simple ear studs, hair tied in a ponytail. Nothing that looked like showing off.

"You should blend, and circulate," Marg said. "Mostly, they'll know you as Cassie."

When Consuela walked into the Mattingleys garden, she was greeted by Gwen Lambert, who introduced her, where necessary, as Cassie from the National Bank. It was a bigger gathering than Connie had expected. As well as the Lamberts, Gwen and her three, there were the Goodmans, the Grants, Josh Gibson and his mother, Sergeant Gower out of uniform, and also the Macphersons and Stevens, whom she had never met. Before Gwen could offer Cassie a glass of cask wine, the younger children were all around her, even Claudia's boys and a young six-year-old named Owen, whom she presumed was a Macpherson.

"Come and join our game, they insisted."

The game involved throwing a bean bag around. If you dropped it, you had to stand on one leg. If you dropped it a second time, you had to put one hand on your head and leave it there. If you fell over or dropped it a third time, as you surely would, you had to pull a face and tell a joke. Cassie was the third one to drop the beanbag and was standing like a flamingo, so when young Owen dropped the bag for the third time and the others didn't laugh at his joke, she was glad to leave the game and console him till his mother, Pamela, came over and introduced herself more personally.

All the time during the game, she had kept looking out for Andy. She didn't want to confront him, but yet it worried her that he wasn't there. Once Owen was calmed down and was accepted back into the game, Pamela asked, "Are you looking for someone?"

"Andrew Thomas, the teacher, I thought he might be here."

"You mean Streuth, that's what he's called in the town. At least all the men call him that."

"Yes, I know. I believe he prefers his friends to call him Andy."

"Are you in that friendship group?"

Should she pretend she hardly knew him? Surely, her friendship with Andrew was well-known in the town as well as her appearances at the tennis club where Andrew was the star player. Instead, she let the question slide and directed a question back at Pamela.

"Is your daughter here? I hear she's a budding literary talent. You can't hide such achievements in this town. I'm sure it's not only my friendship with Andy or my tennis proficiency that is a topic for town gossip."

Pamela took the rebuff in good spirits.

"That's Mandy in the red dress over there with Merle Gibson and the teenagers. While Andrew has been in hospital, Merle has been advising Mandy on the crafting of her illustrated children's story book about a platypus that wants to fly."

"It's fantastic; she has ambition. I hope she is not disappointed. Publishers' rejections may not be about the quality of the work but the likely returns when they do their sums. Dreams can turn to nightmares very easily."

"I believe you were a young tennis star once, had ambitions."

“Yes, that’s a case where it all turned sour. Broke my heart when I had a bad bike accident and wrecked my right wrist. Here in Rainworth, it’s my first time on the court for ten years. I have to learn the game again, retrain my muscles. Re-assess where I want to go with it.”

“Tell me, are you a Catholic?”

“Born into a Catholic family, but un-committed? Went to the Catholic school I believe your daughter will attend next year—the Range Convent back then—just for one year.”

“So you’re tarred with Catholicism?”

“You could say that. It never quite leaves you.”

“You know Andrew is agnostic. Doesn’t believe in God. One afternoon when visiting us, he explained why he was a non-believer and asked Ken and I to defend our loyalty to the Church. It was well intentioned, but quite confronting, I can tell you. Has he challenged you on your beliefs? If not, I’m sure he will.”

Consuela paused, not quite sure how to answer when there was a sudden commotion interrupting them. “Streuth is here! Everybody!” And there was a rush by the men to shake his hand and by several of the women to give him a hug.

“He’s a celebrity amongst this group, especially, the kids and most of the parents. Though my husband, Ken, he’s the local vet and engages with lots of the town and country folk, says Andrew’s not seen that way everywhere in the district. You know about the accident. We all think it was deliberate, just like the attack on you that night at ‘The Blockhouse’?”

"The truck driver has been charged with dangerous driving but not man-slaughter, so Andy told me."

"And the attempted…?"

"Food's ready," Gareth called, and Penny began ushering the children and teens through in a queue to get their meals.

"He's in jail awaiting his fate."

"Our special guests next," Gareth called. "Andy and Cassie, Josh and the Sergeant."

"You go." Pamela insisted, "I'll wait till the end of the queue."

Suddenly, a plate was thrust into Consuela's right hand and an arm went around her waist. It was Andrew.

"Follow Guy. Select what you want from the salad table, and then we go to the barbecue for a choice of the meat. I believe there's steak, sausages, and hamburgers to choose from. All the meat's supplied by Simon Stevens, Gwen Lambert's brother."

They were soon ushered with their meals into a corner of the garden, the five teens around them. Skye joining in.

The questions flowed.

"Sir, when will you be back at school?"

"How's the new Suzuki?"

"We hear that you drove it up in the hills above Virgin Rock? How did it go?"

And the more personal, like,

"Are you and Cassie going steady?"

"Did she spend time with you in Roma?"

"How awful, the rape attack, were you hurt, Cassie?"

"Has Sir consoled you? Hugs and kisses?"

"Do you feel safe in this town? Safe with Sir?"

Before they might ask if he and Connie were sleeping together, Andrew turned the questions on them.

"What school next year for each of you? Except Seb. We know he'll be apprenticed to his father."

After the answers—Guy and Jenny to Emerald High, Skye to Rocky Grammar, and Mandy to The Cathedral College in Rockhampton. Consuela interjected, "The Cathedral College? That's the old Range Convent. I went there for Year 8."

"Why only Grade 8? Didn't you finish school?"

"I went to Spain for over four years and stayed with family there. Attended an international school. All the lessons in English and French."

"And you gave up tennis?"

"In Spain, I took up surfing with my male cousins. Became quite good at it. Riding the waves."

"If you love the surf like Skye's mysterious friend, Scooter, why aren't you living on the Gold Coast rather than here in Rainworth?"

"Cassie doesn't need you prying. She has her reasons!"

"Lucky for you, Sir," was Guy's response, before they all rushed off to attack the sweets that were being put out.

After the meal was over and the plates and left-overs cleared away, Gareth Mattingley invited Councillor Simon Stevens to address the gathering. The Councillor said how pleasing it was to have Andrew and his lovely friend, Cassie, present. "They both have suffered horrible attacks recently, and it is wonderful to have them back smiling and enjoying themselves. On behalf of all present, we especially want to thank the heroes, Josh Gibson for keeping Andrew breathing while trapped in the wreck for three hours, and

Sergeant Gower for rallying the police squad in time to save Cassie from that beastly assault. Please take up a glass. There's beer, wine, champagne, juice, or Coke. We will drink a toast to all four of them."

After that, Connie and Andrew circulated together. It was the polite thing to do. There was something not being said that Connie felt was in the air, a hint of sadness in many voices. It was as if they all suspected this was also an undisclosed farewell party for Andrew. He would leave Rainworth Downs before the year ended. As well what Connie heard most commonly from the parents was how Andrew had helped rescue their children from the terrible moods of the Year 9 year and had eased them into greater respect for themselves—how to ignore any cyber bullying and get over all that agro about parents being unfair. He had promoted time routines and given them sensible reasons why they should turn off all electronic devices at least 30 minutes before going to bed. He'd insisted a good sleep was essential for any scholar.

Everyone felt Skye's outburst and consequent dismissal had been so out of character. She was the one, out of the girls in Andrew's Year 10 classes, who had sailed through the Year 9 year full of self-respect and confidence. It seemed unbelievable—the attack on Grace.

"Look at her now," Gwen Lambert had pointed out, "how she's organising the younger kids to help with the cleanup and dishwashing in the outdoor tubs. Making a game of it."

In Skye's defence, Andrew simply said, "She was in the wrong, but we may not know all the facts. She's still chiding herself for her overreaction."

Merle Gibson interrupted all the conversations by ringing a bell.

"The Year 10s present are going to entertain us with a presentation based on the draft version of Mandy's platypus story. Please be quiet and listen up. They need space to act it out, if you please."

Mandy stepped forward and bowed:

"*Andrew, the platypus, slept too long*
He dreamt he was flying out of his pond.
When his river became just a trickle,
Time to act and not be fickle."

Jenny took over,

"He climbed the bank and grew two wings.
At first, they seemed such clumsy things!"

Each of the five teenagers contributed in turn till they all joined into the final verse:

"He could join the flock of FI-FO geese
And sill forage for worms—his Comet River feast.
A new niche was there for him to fill.
*He became a bird with a...***square-shaped bill***."*

Guy flapped around with a black and white shawl stretched between his extended arms while Seb mimicked the honking sounds of the goose:

"He'd transformed his skin to feathers, too.
Black and white? ...would surely do.
So Andy became a Magpie Goose
This is not a yarn...but...
...the absolute...streuth!"

It was hilarious. A sure step in bonding the adults and juveniles through laughter. A salute to Andrew as well.

When the party broke up, the families and older guest heading home, Penny and Gareth, asked Andrew and Consuela to stay on through the evening and help eat the leftovers. It was a chance to get to know Consuela better, with a thread of matchmaking thrown in. They asked about Spain, about surfing, commented on Andrew's environmental passions, about his dedication to his teaching. All of the talk subconsciously hinting at the difficulty of bridging the cultural gap between the two of them.

Andrew redirected the conversation when it became too personal to proceed further, asking about the presentation night and the legacy it had left in the town folk's attitude and thinking.

"I believe it has been seen as a truly worthwhile educational exercise."

"A new era in education for this town," Penny added. "And they marvelled at the special edition of the newspaper. Not so much the content, but the audacity of it. Giving the students so much voice."

"Adrian should be very proud of that effort. It all read very well, which is great for such a rushed print run."

"And Skye, you made an excellent contribution with your article," Connie added.

"I don't want to be a journalist," Skye replied. "Adrian is welcome to that career. I've decided I am going to study law. Become an environmental lawyer, as I've already told Sir."

"Where will you study?"

"Brisbane, UQ, possibly. ANU in Canberra? Monash in Melbourne? Or maybe Barcelona? Wherever the best courses are."

"I regret now I didn't go on with University study. Only a TAFE certificate in accounting."

"It's not too late—adult entry, if you can finance it."

"Maybe. Creative arts, specialising in photography. I'm thinking about it."

"Connie, I believe you have to give evidence at some kind of police enquiry. At least that's the whisper." It was Gareth making the bold move.

"I didn't think anyone here knew."

"Claudia said you are taking time off later this week, and Marg Bleakley let something slip," Penny covered up so Andrew wasn't seen to be the source of the rumour.

"Is it true?" Andrew asked innocently.

"Yes, Thursday afternoon in Rockhampton. I see this town has its spy network operating."

"Just social media, country style," Skye added. "Will you offer to take Connie into Rocky in your new Suzy, Sir?"

"I'd love to, if Connie will allow me. I am still on sick leave till the 1st of November, that's Tuesday week. My Suzy is available, *Señorita,* for a sexy ride to Rocky."

Connie turned brusquely toward Andrew, "Alana was saying she could come and get me, but hasn't committed. Have you been colluding with her? Is that what's this is all about?"

"Really, Connie, are you rejecting my genuine offer in front of the company here present?"

"No, but I don't like…"

"Don't like what?"

Skye was bursting with laughter. "You idiot, Sir, of course she's saying, 'Yes, thank you'. Don't dance around. Both of you. I hope I never fall seriously in love, if agreeing is going to be so tedious."

She went off to the CD player and the voice of Justin Timberlake singing his song, *'Señorita'* blurted out. Skye began dancing to the slow sensuous beat of the music, and Consuela quickly joined in.

They both beckoned to Andrew to join their writhing bodies, swirling to the rhythm, and he took the floor, reluctantly at first, and then with so much enthusiasm that Penny switched the music on to play again while Skye stepped back and left the lovers to it.

The seal had been made. They couldn't wait to leave, smiling with joy and thanking the Mattingleys profusely for their hospitality.

Chapter 19

Thursday, 27 October 2016

During the drive to Rockhampton, they talked about sharing three days together, staying with Lorae and Alana, visiting the dance school one day or evening, perhaps, a day at the beach at Yeppoon or Emu Park, going surfing.

"Are you going to stay on in Rainworth Downs?" Connie asked. "After what's happened, the crash, the festering hostility towards you in the town that's not likely to go away."

"I'm considering applying for a head of department position at a large high school."

"Where?"

"I called into the school on Monday afternoon, and the regional director was there, visiting from Emerald."

"And?"

"She said the Noosa District High School was advertising for a Head of Humanities with specialist skills in geography teaching. She'd support my application because of all the great effort I'd put in at Rainworth Downs."

"Noosa. Surf, beaches and National Parks. It will suit you, Andrew, though you will miss the Carnarvon Ranges."

“I’m still young for such a promotion. Don’t have much chance. And the school’s not at Noosa, but 20, inland at Cooroy.”

“That has advantages too. Less expensive accommodation.”

“There’s a strong green movement in the Noosa community and two large tennis centres and another at Coolum to the south. Local fixtures and tournaments.”

“I played a junior tournament there once, Noosa Springs Tennis Club. Won the final 6–2. Those were happy days. After I won, I remember my mum bought me a new outfit at a boutique in glamorous Hasting Street. It was a gorgeous blue dress with matching shoes and handbag.”

“I played at the Coolum Tennis club when 15 and lost in the semis. No ‘Streuth’ calls that day.”

There was a pause in the conversation as they entered the outskirts of Rockhampton. Andrew summoning up the courage to pop his proposal.

He took a glance towards Connie when they stopped at the first traffic lights. She was so gorgeous, so desirable.

“If I am lucky and get the position, will you come with me to Noosa?”

“Hold on, our relationship has a long way to go before we live together. That’s a huge decision for me. Truly, *algo para el futuro*. We haven’t even been to bed together, yet?”

“I see, I don’t speak Spanish! And I haven’t passed the sex test.”

“It’s a lovely offer, Andrew,” as Connie kissed his cheek. “Getting through today’s filmed interview is the first hurdle. It will be easier knowing you’re there, outside, supporting me.”

The recorded interviews with the Historical Sexual Assault Unit representatives were being held in a question and answer format in the second of the Rockhampton Magistrate's Courts. There were four other victims listed to testify. Consuela would be first. As an adult, she was not allowed a supporter or legal representation. Andrew and Lorae were required to wait together in the court foyer.

At 1 p.m., a female police officer came out and explained the process and sought to reassure Consuela that all would be fine so long as she told the truth fearlessly. Connie explained she felt confident about speaking out, being forthright, but was nervous about being under the duress of the formal process, and the possibility of trick questions from left field. The police officer tried to allay the fears, but Connie was not convinced.

"If they believe me, all of my story, it still won't be enough to convict him."

"Darling, that's why they have other witnesses or victims. They have listed five today, and they may have more in other locations. It's all about building a strong case. Do you recognise any of the other names on this list?"

"I don't think so, unless this one…Glenda Edwards, of course, my roommate at that Gympie tennis camp. The one sent to hospital with acute appendicitis."

Andrew tried not to show his guilty smile. There was a confession he had yet to make to Connie.

"It will be interesting," he said, barely audibly, "to hear what she knows about Gavin Davis."

When called at 1:15 p.m., Consuela gave both her mother and Andrew a hug. They each whispered their own words of encouragement in her ear, then, feeling lonely and abandoned, she followed the officer into the courtroom.

Andrew and Lorae sat quietly for, perhaps, 30 minutes, each immersed in their own thoughts till Andrew spoke.

"My Dad told me once, that the worst time he ever had in his life was sitting in a waiting room at the Roma Hospital while my mother gave birth to me. He kept thinking about all the dreadful things that could go wrong."

"While your mother no doubt was in agony. Small price a father has to pay, I can tell you. Consuela's was a difficult birth, I screamed and groaned for hours. Alana's had been a much easier delivery, but Consuela was a problem child."

"I don't believe there were any complications with my birth as it turned out, other than the terror, I guess, every first-time mother feels. But my dad was emotional the day before my graduation when he said, 'If you had died at birth, Andrew, I could have lived with that. But I don't know what I would have done if your mother had died.' They weren't married then, and I realise he would have felt so shamefully guilty."

"Gavin Davis should have felt more than guilty for what he did to ruin my daughter's life, her talent, her ambitions. I hope the dread of being found out has haunted him all these years, but I suspect it hasn't."

They were suddenly interrupted.

"Hello, Andrew,' a tall young woman, dressed in maternity wear and obviously pregnant, stood beside him. "And it is Misses Alverez, isn't it?"

Andrew, jumped to his feet, to appraise the source of the voice. "Glenda, and you obviously know Lorae."

"All the girls in the junior tennis circles around Rockhampton knew Misses. Alverez. We all wanted to grow into a lady with such beauty, style, and elegance. Tennis aside, we loved the way you looked, Lorae, so magnificent without being a slave to fashion. So I guess you are waiting for Consuela to come out from her interview session."

"Yes, she's been in there for more than 40 minutes."

"I'm scheduled for 2:15 p.m., so I guess they won't keep her a lot longer. So why are you here, Andrew? Don't tell me you and Consuela are an item?"

"Not exactly…just close friends."

Lorae was forthright, no point to adding to the rumour mill. "Since her suicide attempt, I guess you heard that news on local radio and read it in the Rocky Bulletin—Connie has been working at Rainworth Downs where Andrew teachers."

"You were in a car crash, weren't you, not so long back, Andy. The bulletin covered that story, as well. Some huge mine truck ran you off a narrow country road. Weren't you badly injured?"

"I was lucky to get out alive. A fellow tennis player arrived just in time to stop me from choking on my own vomit, and keeping me alive, waiting three hours for the air rescue chopper."

"That would have been an agonising wait?"

"I was unconscious, knew nothing about it. Not like this wait which is driving me up the wall."

"Then the relationship is serious."

"Some emotions, you can't hide. So were you also assaulted by Davis?"

"Not exactly, just the repeated sexual innuendo, the slaps on bum, hands on your thighs, suggestive massages. He was a good coach, but he took liberties. Mums and the female coaches let him get away with it. Any reports to Queensland Tennis authorities were dismissed because he was getting results for Queensland Junior tennis."

"Connie hid what happened at that Gympie camp from us."

"I was sick with appendicitis, as you no doubt know, I tried to warn her about Coach, but was rushed off to hospital. She was so young, at least two years younger than any others in the group. And on her day, I believe, she could beat all of us. She was brilliant on the court, and so aggressive."

"Lorae and I hope that fighting spirit has emerged in the interview."

"How come you two know each other?"

"We were at the same University for a year—UQ in Brisbane. Played some tennis together on the Uni courts."

Any further explanation was halted by the court doors opening and Connie running out to be hugged by her mum. Nothing more was said except they wished Glenda well and departed.

Consuela travelling to the Alverez's home in her mother's car, with Andrew following in his Suzi.

That evening, Andrew lay beside Connie on the double-bed in her room. Lorae sat beside them, and Alana stood by the door, listening.

"It was awful. Humiliating. Demeaning. They weren't satisfied with the events of the tennis camp. They grilled me about my non-existent sex life, about how much I knew at

13, about my knowledge of dildos and vibrators, about my sex education, about pleasuring myself, about the difference between sports massage and erotic massage, about my fondness for the Coach. Then, about him grooming me and when I believe physical abuse becomes rape. They went on and on. One box of tissues was not nearly enough. I was shattered by the end of it. Giving birth to a child couldn't be worse than that."

"And your depression and the suicide attempt?" Alana asked.

"All that, too. Whom I turned to for help. My psychiatrist."

"And Uncle Climent? No doubt they dismissed that as family. Not professional help."

"They said he was best left out of the picture, or Davis's defence might say the whole story was contrived by the family."

Lorae protested, "That was really unfair. Doubting Climent's professionalism."

"But they had a point," Andrew added. "None of us want the fucking bastard getting off over some technical argument about conflict of interest."

Connie was weeping again, squeezing Andrew's hand tightly and turning to look him in the eyes.

"Just knowing I had support outside was important."

"We were there stressed, but cheering for you all the time."

"Was that Glenda Edwards there when I came out?"

"Yes, and I'd say six months pregnant. She looked lovely. Strong-willed, I'd say, and in command of her life. Ready to testify against Davis."

Andrew had the final word, before they left Connie to have a quiet rest.

"Knowing Glenda, she will sink the nails in. Hammering home the facts regarding the liberties Gavin Davis took. Making it clear about his pattern of behaviour. Not just Glenda, but other girls too from that era are having their say. Grilling you all, crosschecking everything may seem harsh treatment, but it will result in undeniable evidence of repeated abuse, physical or emotional, when his case goes to court."

Streuth, he thought, as he walked with Lorae and Alana into the kitchen, *seeing Glenda. Consuela still doesn't know about my past association with her. Potential for another ball to be hit through my chest.*

"I hope you don't mind having me here for three days. Consuela said I could sleep on a fold-out settee in the lounge area. Is that okay?"

Alana and Lorae exchanged smiles.

"You won't offend, Andrew, if Connie would like you in her bedroom."

"I suspect Mum is saying we wouldn't be offended," Alana added.

"I couldn't, without Connie's invitation. I realise she's a…a *'novice'*. It would be a huge step for her."

"She's well read on sex, and I know she watches some porn."

"That's a little too much information, Alana, for now. I'll get on with preparing the meal, and you can see to Andrew's arrangements in the lounge. You're a good man, Andrew, and Connie needs your compassionate approach. If she really loves you, she'll come around and even realise, may I say, that sex in a trusted relationship is good for both the body and the mind."

Alana had it all planned.

"First up, let Connie have a full day, admitting to her post traumatic stress. That won't be easy. Then, tomorrow evening, Andy, we are taking you both to Mum's dance school for night's 8 p.m. session. I'll teach you the Salsa, and Connie will get so jealous, she will have to join in with another partner, and then I'll force her to swap. You'll see how wonderful she is on the dance floor. The dancing will get very erotic and romantic."

"I'll make a total fool of myself,"

"No, you won't! It's a bit like playing tennis. A good serve is all about rhythm. You'll be clumsy at first but then you'll soon get into the swing and love it."

"What else are you and your mother planning?"

"A night at the Endeavour Inn, Emu Park. Balcony room with views. Close to the best surfing on the Yeppoon coast. Here's my phone, make the booking now!"

"She might not accept my invitation."

"Put on the charm. She'll suspect Mum and I are complicit. But you play it as if it's totally your proposal, like a first serious date. Plead, if you have to, but don't accept a, *'No!'*."

"Are you familiar with the Bryan Adams' song, *'Heaven'*? If you do, sing it to her at the motel. Or I can lend you my CD player and you can play it to her in her room late tomorrow night tonight, after we are back here from the dancing."

Alana sang…

"I've been waitin' for so long
For somethin' to arrive
For love to come along..."

They blundered through the next five lines, not confident of the words, then ending together with,

"I'm findin' it hard to believe
We're in heaven."

Chapter 20

Friday, 28 October 2016

They checked in as Mister and Misses Thomas. When he took the key, Andrew clasped it as if it were a precious jewel. It was a passport to intimacy with a woman such as he had never previously known. It wasn't as if he was a virgin. He assumed Consuela realised that. Yet neither was he experienced in a way that prepared him for the present situation.

He had known Glenda Edwards during his second year at the University of Queensland. At the lookout above Virgin Rock, he had wanted to interrupt and tell Consuela that—that they had played together on the UQ courts and had dated for a while. But after Connie had completed her harrowing story, he felt it more discrete to say nothing.

Glenda had arrived at Women's College as a freshman and posted a notice, '*Tennis practice partner wanted!*' So he had teamed up with her on and off the court. One semester break, they went with six other Uni friends to stay for a week of bushwalking at the Binna Burra Lodge on the edge of the Lamington National Park. The others had coupled up, so one night he found himself alone with Glenda in one of the girls' cabins. They were both virgins.

Hesitant. Till Glenda produced a condom packet and asked, "Are you game?" And went on, "The other girls are goading me to join their ranks." He was eager enough. She was quite attractive. Desirable. He couldn't refuse such a bold invitation.

The mating was awkward, right from when Glenda had to help him roll on the sheath. They never completely undressed, fearing interruption, while he quickly realised how inept he was at exciting her. He became impatient, while she remained understanding. Too much so, and he came quickly, exploding into her, withdrawing abruptly, the deed done. They lay together laughing, both feeling silly. "You didn't orgasm," he remembered saying. "Sorry, I have a lot to learn."

She had replied, "Never mind, Andy, so do I. It was sweet of you. Another time we will have more foreplay. Learn the joy of sex." The relationship ended when Glenda returned to Rocky to help nurse her sick mother, who had cervical cancer. She finished her Uni studies at Central Queensland University.

Now, here he was alone in the motel room with Connie. They slumped down together on the queen bed—enough room, so that they did not need to touch.

"You're quiet, pensive." Connie said.

"I don't know what shots to play. I can tell you how beautiful you are; how I loved dancing with you; how everything about you excites me; or how well I'm sure you coped with the recorded interview yesterday; and how the historical assault officers would have been impressed with your damming indictment of Coach Davis and Queensland Tennis. And…it's not really how I want to play."

"And the rally you want to play is about sex, intimate sex?"

"Yes, the desire I have…it is like the nervous energy I remember before playing in a tournament final. You just want to bring it on. Then, on the court, you rush things, forget your pre-match strategy, over hit your drives, double fault going for the big serves."

"You know I have my fears. I'm thinking and doing the same at the other end of the court. I don't want to be rushed. We could wait. Call this match off. Consummate our relationship near Mooloolong below Cave Hill, or at Major Mitchell's beloved Salvator Rosa…perhaps, in December."

She rolled into his waiting arms. Kissed him on the cheek, then gently on the lips. He was visiting heaven. True to the song. Yet there was not enough light to make it safe to play. Not the right music in the air."

"Let's go to the beach," Connie said. "I'll wear my bikini, and we can swim together, dancing around in the music of the sea. Rekindle the joy of our Salsa from last night. Only this time…dancing just for us. I want you to forget darling Skye and her classmates, all the girls you've ever taken to bed. I want you absolutely to myself these three days."

Connie hopped up and rummaged around in her suitcase for swimwear and went to the bathroom. Andrew waited while lying on the bed, wondering when if ever he should tell Connie about Glenda. Then, he stood up and changed into his swimmers and a T-shirt.

When Connie emerged, he was delighted, flabbergasted—the glowing psychedelic colours of the bikini, the long legs, the body shape, the curves. He had previously seen so little of her skin beyond the face and neck or below the knees, that he found himself wanting to perv, to drink it all in.

Connie handed him her sunscreen tube, “Do my back please, and I’ll do yours.”

It was the first time he had touched her bare flesh except for her lovely face or when holding hands together. He was delirious with the joy of the simple task, noticing the perfection of the light bronze skin, the one small mole on the left shoulder.

“Gentle,” she said. “Enjoy the moment.”

And before long, he had the pleasure of her attentiveness, both back and chest. Joking about his lack of body hair, his muscles, his little tits. There was her smiling face, her breasts and cleavage up close, and the tingling sensation of her fingers stroking down his body.

Walking to the beach, Connie kept her beach coat closed, her large sun hat pulled down towards her sunglasses. She didn’t want to be recognised by other swimmers. She directed them past the famous Singing Ship landmark on the headland and down over the rocks to the Ladies Beach, enclosed between two small rocky outcrops. The tide was in and the water well up the beach.

“The breeze is a little cold,” Andrew remarked. “Do you still want to swim?”

“Of course, I do!” And Connie dropped her towel, beach hat, beach coat, thongs, and sunnies, at the base of the rocks, and took off across the sand and into the water, assuring herself Andrew would follow.

He watched her glide over the beach—her athleticism, the fluidness of her movements so alluring in themselves.

How could he wait till December? How he wished he could know every part of her body. Her shell-like ears under the black hair, the curve of her neck as it joined her shoulders, the beautiful mounds of flesh that formed her breasts, the sensitive nipples, the tummy button, the pubic mysteries currently hidden by the tantalisingly small bikini bottom. Then, he rushed in, grabbing her hand as they ducked into the waves together.

After the swim and a while sunbaking, they made their way back to the motel, on the way checking out venues for their evening meal and finding nothing to their taste. Connie showered first and came out bare breasted with a large towel wrapped around her waist. Andrew hurried into the shower, more there to masturbate than to wash—a release of sexual tension, not once, but three times in all. When he came out of the bathroom, Connie was dressing to go out to dinner. She wanted to brush her hair and to do her makeup, and he wanted to watch. She explained the use of colour correction, foundation, eyeshadow, blush, and highlighter using a fan brush, and then the choice of a lipstick—a reddish tone for this occasion. Carefully done and efficient. Then out at the bed she pulled on a mid-length black dress with a lacy top and a hidden zip at the back which she asked him to close. She put a small flower broach in her hair but let it flow free. Andrew finished his own dressing, slacks and a blue shirt, knowing how he would feel so underdressed in the company of such an elegant woman.

They decided to drive north to a restaurant at Yeppoon that Alana had recommended. There, they were placed at a table, overlooking the lights of Rosslyn Bay. They ordered two glasses of white wine rather than a full bottle; and chose the barramundi from the menu, Connie with salad and Andrew with vegetables—each noting the other's preference. They talked about Lorae and the dance school, the success of her business; about Connie's growing up in Rockhampton compared with Andrew's boyhood in Roma; about films and books they had loved. It was all small talk, and when the waitress asked about sweets, they declined, both anxious to be back at the motel where the queen bed awaited them.

Once the door was locked, they embraced and showered each other with kisses, soft kisses around the neck, the ears, the forehead, the eyes; both gentle and vigorous on the lips, again and again.

"You may undress me," Connie offered, "as I undress you. One garment at a time."

Andrew sang the lyrics of *'Heaven'* as well as he could remember them all from the previous night, and Connie joined in till completely naked. They pulled back the covers and flopped together on the bed.

"You're shaved," he said. "I didn't expect that, the lack of pubic hair."

"You haven't seen a nude pussy? So much part of our modern world. Waxing and laser clinics are common now."

"You have left some tufts."

"It was Alana's idea, just a little bush left. She said you'd like it. She was the one who dared me to do the shave. She helped me first thing this morning. Are you disappointed?"

"No-o. It's a beautiful sight. Thank you."

"Take a closer look. Don't touch. Not yet."

Andrew knelt between Consuela's legs. Leaning down to see the outer lips glistening. His index finger and thumb itching to fold back the lips like flower petals and explore, his tongue ready to follow, to taste the love nectar.

Connie's memory flashed back to the dildo at the tennis camp. She thought she had put it behind her, that terrible experience, yet it was there now, raw in her mind.

"Enough!" she suddenly shouted, pushing him away and closing her legs tightly.

Reluctantly he moved up the bed and straddling her, his knees beside her hips. She was shaking with grief, yet he left her be, wondering what to do, what to say.

"How can I love you, sexually, without touching with my fingers or my penis? Connie, you have to choose or end it here. I can't be strung along like your surfer boy in Spain. Paulo was it?"

"I'm sorry, Andy. Just be patient with me."

"I am trying hard, but my only release will be to go to the bathroom and masturbate, or spill my load here on your naked body in the bed."

"Go ahead and do it, I don't care but not down there, not in the vagina."

And he did it. Suddenly, losing control. Thrusting and jerking, the seminal fluid spurting out over her chest, some running down into her umbilicus and even on to wet the tuft of pubic hair. He couldn't stop, a fountain of creamy liquid. And Connie accepted it as if it was her punishment for denying him. For denying herself.

Andrew rolled away from her, humiliated.

Connie rushed to the bathroom, with Andrew calling to her back, "Sorry, I'm so sorry!"

He heard the shower running and her loud sobs above the splash of the shower water.

She had left the door ajar, and he entered cautiously, giving a little cough so she would know he wanted to be there with her. He had expected rejection, yet she opened the shower door and invited him in. He watched as she scrubbed at the offending gooeyness till she was satisfied. It was all gone and then she melted into his arms, the warm shower splashing over both of them, easing their pain, the embarrassment. He went to speak, to apologise again, but Connie said, "Shush. It's all my fault. I love you, Andrew, even though it may not appear that way right now."

Eventually, Andrew turned off the shower and they dried each other down, Andrew leaving Connie to attend to her wet hair.

"Would you like some coffee?" he called out.

"No, thanks. There's a choice of something stronger in the mini bar. Rum and coke sounds in order."

They dressed in their nightwear and sat at the small table, enjoying the drink.

"I have something to tell you," Andrew said, "about me and Glenda Edwards."

"Oh, Andy. Don't tell me you're the father of her child."

"No way! Till the surprise outside the hearing at the courthouse I hadn't seen her for seven years. Since university."

"So. Go on."

"Glenda arrived at UQ in 2008 to commence her studies. I was in my second year…"

It took nearly an hour to tell Consuela about the relationship, the apology for not telling her sooner; the first sex in the cabin at Binna Burra lodge; how he and Glenda got accustomed to sharing a room for the weekend when playing at country tennis tournaments—Toowoomba, Maryborough, Miami on the Gold Coast. In response to her questioning, he told about the positions they tried and how Glenda liked to be on top; and also about their oral sex indulgences and them watching porn together. It was his time fronting up to an inquisitor, merciless in her questions. Andrew needed the release, he agonised and squirmed, crying audibly till he got through it, with the python in his pants writhing with urgency.

"Well, Mister Nice Guy, Sex Stud, dry your eyes," Consuela said, standing up and provocatively throwing off her night wear. "If the plain Glenda Edwards could coerce you into her bed, so can I."

She lay down on the white bed sheet and spread her legs, crooning with joy. He was with her in a flash his swollen penis searching for entry.

It was smooth, it was lustful, it was the heaven they so much desired.

They copulated three times, all in the missionary position, each time lasting longer than the last with Andrew becoming more and more vigorous till each explosive climax released them and they could lay quietly, enjoying the reassurance of kisses.

After the first time, Connie said, "It's okay, Andy, I'm on the pill."

After the second time, Andy said, I'd be happy if you have no protection, You're mine. I'm yours."

"Any child from our union would be blessed."

That was the limit of the conversation till sometime after the third event when they lay exhausted and calm, Connie said, “Listen to that beautiful sound. It’s the wind in the rigging of the Singing Ship, up on the headland. It reminds me of the whistling kite. That first outing we had together. The bird circling above us. Blessing our union.”

Chapter 21

Sunday, 30 October 2016

They were driving back to Rainworth Downs when Consuela asked Andrew what he was thinking about.

"I start back at school on Tuesday, and my first lesson will be with the year 10 geography class."

"I knew it, back in the school master role."

"They will sense a change. Suspect I have committed myself elsewhere. That their progress, their subject knowledge, their results, are no longer my major concern. That in a way they have been downgraded, despite the success of the Comet River study and their presentation night."

"You can't downgrade their effort. Surely, they all deserve an A."

"At the end of term, it would be improper to award ten A results. I will be accused of favouritism, of distorted judgment."

"Well, it's not for me to interfere, but surely 50% graded A is reasonable, knowing their dedication."

"It's my worry. I'll endeavour to be fair and gracious. Let's talk about something else."

"When do you finish at school? We have to live apart till at least then."

"Breakup is officially the 9th of December, but the year 10s will be allowed to finish a week earlier."

"Can we spend the November weekends away? We could go camping. Show me the Consuelo Tableland, go back to Cave Hill, celebrate our love at Salvator Rosa...anywhere you desire."

"Tomorrow, I'll apply for the Noosa District High School position. If I am lucky and get it, I will leave Rainworth almost immediately the term ends. Certain elements in the town will cheer, especially the mining interests. There could be a last hurrah, a farewell day, perhaps, at the tennis club on December 10. Then, I'll head to Roma for time with family and on to Noosa and look for suitable accommodation. What about you?"

"No promises. Maybe a trial of living together in the New Year. I might have to appear in court in Rockhampton twice—once regarding the rape attempt, and once if Gavin Davis is charged. I'll have a clearer head after that."

"I might yet have a court appearance over the crash, that's probably in February."

"Andy, what about the camping trips?"

"Of course, it's our best opportunity for private time. To get to know each other better."

"These couple of days have been great, that was more in my world near the sea. Camping in close contact with nature, that's your world. I need to share that with you. Test the compatibility of our values. The intertwining like a helix."

"Perhaps, this next weekend at tennis. I'll try my best hobbling around the court. It's the right thing to do. That leaves three weekend camping trips. First time for Suzi here, into the wilds."

"It's for me, Andy, not the car. With the love of your life. That's the test. It's not the sex test, that's over. You passed several times, five different positions, all enjoyable. It's the love test."

"I suspect, despite my efforts, you haven't yet climaxed explosively, you haven't reached the full joy, the screaming out of the porn videos."

"Alana says that may not happen till I have the courage to invite you to go down on me. She keeps texting me about it. How cunnilingus is the delicious sweet of sex. A woman needs the entree of foreplay, the main course of robust penetration, and the delight of oral sex to make the meal complete."

"I'm looking forward to it when you gain the courage."

Tuesday, 1 November 2016

The whole class stood to welcome back Mister Thomas, as he arrived walking with barely a hobble.

"Thank you for the welcome. Be seated. That is your cue, Skye."

Skye came to the front of the room, then asked Clare to join her. The apology was wholeheartedly earnest, not just to Clare but to the whole class.

"Now, Jane come forward so I can congratulate you for your equestrian triumph and for being appointed school captain."

"And Danielle, congratulations on riding your first race. You didn't run a place yet it must have been a thrill."

Guy was to his feet.

"Do I have to congratulate you Guy for becoming a stunt pilot of a helicopter?"

"No, Sir, I'm still adjusting to the feel of wings. Like a baby goose. But can we play the film we made of the presentation night. It's been edited by Jonathan. Takes 45 minutes."

"No! You can project it for me in the hall at lunch break, if you like. Now, you all have work to do on your river study. It's your last assignment to determine your final marks, together with a short-written exam, so it's important to get on with it and do a good job."

He watched as they settled into their working pairs. Skye with Jonathan on the Tigris-Euphrates study, Mandy with Clare on the Mekong, Jenny and Seb investigating the Yukon, Jane and Guy studying the Zambezi, and Josie with Danielle on the Paraguay. Then, he sat down with Jenny and Seb.

Jenny spoke up for help. "We've found so many articles on the internet and have made pages of notes. Seb and I am not sure what to do next."

"It's a seminar type presentation, not too elaborate, and a written presentation."

Then, Seb went on, "If we just use passages from the sources, it's going to be plag…"

"That's true, avoiding plagiarism is important. Set up your major headings—catchment area physical details, the people of the area, the economic exploitation, harnessing the river for water, power, irrigation. That will be enough."

He circulated and checked on the other groups.

At the end of the session, Andrew addressed the whole class. "Have confidence in what you're doing. We will start seminar presentations next Tuesday, two weeks today, 15th of November. Two pairs that day and three on the Thursday. Your test will be on the 22nd of November, based on the topics and geographical understanding you have developed this term."

"Sir," Guy was on his feet again. "Don't we all deserve an A for the Comet Dam project?"

"Guy, much as I'd like to do that. It would not be fair to those who made the biggest contribution, and have shown the greatest range of geographical skills. As an example, hands up those who expect they will get an A in science?"

Mandy and Jonathan's hands went up.

"It's likely we can add Skye to that, and one or two from the eight non-geography students. There will be no more than that awarded in English or maths, I'm sure that by now you realise pretty well where you stand."

Mandy Macpherson cornered him outside.

"Sir, the full class report on the Comet Dam study is complete with photographs as well. We just want you to add a foreword so it can be printed and placed in the library."

"I'm told by Skye and Mister James, what a fine job you've done as editor. I'd like to read the report first, and I'll have my piece ready for next Tuesday. I hope a copy will go to the Shire archives and 'The Blockhouse' library collection. Any family that wants it as a memento should also receive a copy."

"Sir, I'm sorry about Skye, they were nasty to her."

“Mandy, Skye has benefitted from the experience. We shouldn’t think we can be top dog all the time.”

“We all love you, Sir, in our own way. You’ve been the best. Skye was just the one who was more overt about it. You should remember her schoolgirl crush as a compliment from the whole class.”

“Thanks, Mandy, that was well-expressed even if it bends the truth a little.”

Chapter 22

Saturday, 10 December 2016

"There's a text on my phone from Skye."

"I have one too, but wondered if I should tell you."

Andrew and Connie had just set up camp at the Salvator Rosa campsite in the western section of Carnarvon National Park. On the two-hour drive out from Rainworth Downs, Andy had talked about the final results he'd awarded in the geography class. It irked Consuela that he wouldn't let it go, ranking the students, what amounted to a self-critique of his teaching achievements. She was having to realise, that if she wanted to love and live with this man, she had to accept that the success he had achieved with the Year 10 geography class was a pinnacle achievement in his teaching life—it would stand out for him in years to come like the spectacular Mt. Mooloolong spire did in the landscape.

Andrew spoke on over the noise of the engine. "Josie was easy, overjoyed at her C rating. Jane was not so happy with her B minus, partly the result of failing the short exam. I think her mind is all a flutter. She has announced she's going steady with Guy, though I'm not sure Guy's fully in tune. He's not into horse riding, for a start. I awarded an A rating to Skye, Mandy, Jonathan, and Jenny, and B plus or

B to the others. They thought I was a little tough but accepted my decisions.

"The whole Year 10 cohort had a great time at their breakup party, hosted by the Macpherson family last weekend. As you know, I went along. Since it was away from the school and the rules that might apply, there were hugs all round. They congratulated me and wished me well with the move to Noosa, saying the town was losing a champion. The girls all wanted to know whether you were going with me, and I responded that that was private business."

After that, Andrew's and Connie's conversation centred on themselves. They reminisced about the night of Connie's 23rd birthday. They'd spent it on Conseulo Tableland above the spectacular Carnarvon Gorge. How it was amusing that he, Andy, had been on top of both Consuela and Consuelo as they indulged in the pleasure of birthday sex; and how they had been caught in dense fog and then rain as they tramped out. Andy had said, "That one must learn to enjoy the environment in all it moods," and Connie had remarked, that he had a funny idea of what constitutes joy.

Their night in the moonlight, after they had climbed Cave Hill together, was far more pleasurable. Just on sunset, a whistling kite had perched on a tree by their campsite and whistled away, as the moon rose and flooded the valley and hills in soft light. Their lovemaking was all the more sweet for the bird's presence. The sunrise next morning, lighting up the temple of Mt. Mooloolong, was truly spectacular. Connie's camera shutter was very busy. She had taken over a hundred photos over the two days and was proud at having dispatched a selection with a short article to both the *'Wild and Great Walks'* magazines.

"So what does Skye write?" Andrew asked.

"You first, Andy."

He read, *'I wish you both every happiness (happiness as an emoji face). I remember being at Salvator Rosa and climbing up to the Spyglass with you when I was eleven. You were in your first year here. It's a (happy face again) memory.'*

"So the little vixen had her eyes on you way back."

"She was just a kid out here camping with her parents and Adrian that winter break, and I had been exploring for some aboriginal art sites in the Upper Nagoa—sites that Grahame Walsh had located and written about in his book, *'Carnarvon and Beyond'*. It was nice meeting up with the Mattingleys in the wild. Skye was such a terror back then. Full of energy. We all went swimming together at the junction of the Nagoa and Luisa Creek, where the stream is the deepest. Beautiful white sand and crystal-clear water."

"Here's what she texted to me."

'Consuela, I hope you join Andy in Noosa. Love to be invited to the wedding.'

"She's back to being her own precocious self. Taking liberties."

"Forget Skye, I have some news I've been hiding from you. Now's the right time to tell you. I've resigned from the bank two week ago. I finished up yesterday. The move was not unexpected by Mister Smithson, nor Gloria. I'm hoping to go freelance with photography and short journal articles. I'm free to go on to Roma with you, if you agree. Your parents already know to expect me."

Sunday, 11 December 2016

Andrew and Connie had explored the Wagga Ridge area on the Saturday afternoon, so Connie could photograph two more large sandstone pinnacles Andy named *'The Sentinel'* and *'The Elephant'*. They spent the night around a campfire, swapping stories and information with a group of seven bushwalkers who were packing up to leave on the Sunday after a full week at Salvator Rosa.

"You must go up the Nagoa past the Louisa junction and climb up into the Amphitheatre area. That's where you get the best views of the *'Three Sisters'* formation and Mount Pythagoras from the west."

One of the party was an experienced nature photographer, and he and Consuela spent some time comparing their cameras and what they could achieve with the right settings and lighting. She made notes from the conversation, notes which she would carry with her the next day when bushwalking.

"We'll leave Spyglass Peak till tomorrow and spend the day out in the upper Nagoa and the Amphitheatre area," Andrew suggested as they set off for a full day's tramping and exploring. The birdlife was prolific though elusive to photograph, and the summer flowers were not at their best, baring the rock orchids. Nevertheless, Consuela found much to photograph. For a lunch spot, they found a grassy bank beside an inviting pool at a meander bend in the Nagoa and stripped down to swim and splash together naked in a waist deep pool.

"This is the way to enjoy *'The Nature'* on a hot summer's day, like Finnish families, bathing while enjoying the scenic precincts in the forest." Yet his eyes rarely wandered around to take in the environment, fixed so persistently on the beautiful lithe woman who played and splashed in the cool water and then sunbaked beside him. He took his own bevy of photos with his compact camera and more, under instruction, to achieve the best portrait snaps of Connie using her Nikon.

In the afternoon, up on The Amphitheatre ridge, the photographs were all of landscapes, the telephoto lens and the wide angle proving their value. “Who, I wonder, since the artists in Major Mitchell’s party, has been here to paint?” Connie asked herself as they walked past Mt. Pythagoras and back to camp. “The scenery is truly magnificent. Andrew, what was it that Mitchell wrote?”

‘It was a discovery worth the toils of a pilgrimage…I never saw anything in nature come so near these creations of genius and imagination.’ Andrew silently thought how the words could apply to the beautiful Consuela Alverez whose hand he grasped tightly.

That evening, being alone, they lay out under the stars, too exhausted from the hiking and the heat to engage in sex. They were content, simply being together in consort with the natural world.

“We have never talked about religion, what we believe,” Andrew said by way of conversation. “Why do you think, we are here?”

Here we go, Consuela thought, then replied without conviction, “Only God knows.”

“You don’t still believe in God, surely, after what you’ve been through.”

“I was brought up in a Catholic family where it seemed compulsory, though none of us went to church except on special occasions.”

“And life after death?”

“Really, Andrew I don’t think about it. You could say being here with you is life after death for me. It is more wonderful than I could ever have hoped for less than a year ago.”

“I’m only asking to tease out what we have in common, metaphysically. To me my faith is not in God. It is in the remarkable science of life and evolution. There is a growing agnostic fraternity that believes we are here by chance not certainty, the result of an infinite chain of cosmic events.”

“You’re going far too deep for me.”

Having started, Andrew had a compelling urge to persist. He rolled over towards Connie and looked into her eyes, those close glittering stars that enchanted him.

“Let’s address this another way… See all those stars. In a planet circling one of them there could be life, even equivalent to our so-called *‘intelligent life’*. If so, I wonder what they are thinking as they look out on the cosmos? Are they surmising that there is a creator being who is responsible for all that they know and see. Do they have a holy book, full of what atheists would say are spurious answers?”

Connie remained silent, waiting for Andrew to continue as she knew he would.

“Surely, they are not that silly, for a creator concept only induces another question, about who or what created the creator.”

“As I see it,” Connie responded. “Most religion is about the vision of an after-life for members of the chosen species, forgetting life includes so much more…plants, animals, micro-organisms, viruses. Now, can we let this rest and just enjoy the sight of the stars and the rising moon.”

Andrew rolled back away, yet he had to make one last thrust to see if Connie shared his wavelength, his vision of the meaning of being.

“If, say we have children, and I die suddenly in an accident, what do you say to a five-year-old daughter who is asking, *‘where’s my Daddy gone?’*.”

“I would probably say Daddy’s gone up to be in heaven.”

“The *‘up to’* has a problem for me. I would say, come and look at the night sky. It’s likely at least one speck out there in the great universe has an intelligent child asking the same question. There may be more in the cosmos where their stars are too far away for us to detect. Mummy’s body has gone back to be a little part of the system that drives all existence in the cosmos. She is helping to nourish new life here or somewhere else in our universe.

“Streuth! She will be thinking I have a nutty father.”

“My answer to that is to say, not only am I nutty, indeed all life is a somewhat bizarre phenomenon.”

Connie turned onto her knees ready to get to her feet and go off to the toilet.

“As you have eloquently explained, Sir, it is by fortune, bizarre or not, that we are camping here together, alone in this beautiful part of our planet Earth. We are blessed, wherever the blessing comes from. And I wish that it continues like a never-ending song of joy, a whistling kite or a Singing Ship monument providing the music."

Connie stood and went to move off, "When I come back, and I've brushed my teeth, you may help me into the sleeping bag and cuddle me to sleep, but no more talk of metaphysics."

Chapter 23

Monday, 12 December 2016

Andrew and Consuela lunched beside the Belinda Spring—the sparkling spring water running out through lush ferns and sedges down a bank into the sandy bed of Louisa Creek. Earlier, they had climbed up to the arch on Spyglass Peak while Connie had taken more photographs of the countryside and carefully focused close-up pics of the white and yellow wildflowers scattered through the forest. Now, as they ate, lorikeets flocked around a clump of nearby gum trees in flower, azure kingfishers darted along the creek bank, and monarch butterflies delighted with their colourful acrobatics.

"Andrew," Connie spoke cautiously, "this will be difficult… That discussion last night about spiritual beliefs and faith, communicating hard truths with a child."

"Yes?"

"It has made me think that the euphoria of our present love and our sexual bonding is not enough to hold us together forever. We're unlikely to ride this wave of joy for more than a year or two. Then, other factors will become more apparent. Culturally we have many differences, and different ambitions as well. With your promotion and job security, you are ready for your own home, marriage, and a family. Please understand…and I'm trying to put this kindly, but I'm not ready for a settled life."

Andrew looked away. A maddening shudder swept down through his body all the way to his toes. These were words he didn't want to hear. They went against all his future hopes.

"You have been wonderful for me. You have released me from the distressing confines of my murky pond, saved me from myself; and now, unfortunately for you, I know that like the platypus I want to fly. There is just one more test, a game I need to play before I'll feel the full benefit of growing wings. Sharing your values, your agnosticism, is not a problem, but like most young women in Australia today, an independent life and career will have priority as I fly free."

"Where is this heading?" His voice anxious with the fear of a split.

"I'll come to Noosa with you. Make it a base while I study journalism and creative arts in photography or film—study at the University of the Sunshine Coast or online. I'm sure living together will be very pleasurable, full of tender love and sexual delights, but I can't give a promise to share your ongoing desires and dreams.

"You're saying I'll have to play well, very strategically, to have a chance of holding on to you."

"I'm saying I'm unsure where my new-grown wings will ultimately take me—Sydney, Paris, New York, back to Spain? Even into someone else's arms."

"If that happens, it'll be a dreadful blow. A ball through the gut. Unbearable! Soul destroying!"

“I have faith that you’d recover. We both have, already, from horrific events. Indeed, before long you might find someone else. Another Glenda? A grown-up Skye?”

Andrew couldn’t hold back his ire. She had stung him again though he still held his resolve. Despite the grave implications of the future Connie had outlined, he could see she was in a happy mood. There was this glint in her eyes he hadn’t seen before. She was nervously excited.

“You said there was one more test for you to pass—some kind of game. Not sure what it is, but it’s your serve. I’ll receive, if that’s what you want? You might end up hating me forever if I don’t play.”

Connie blushed, her face lighting up with a broad smile.

“Look what Alana sent me for my birthday,” she said while unwrapping a parcel from her day pack.

Andrew realised immediately. It was a dildo-shaped vibrator—*Femplay* brand, similar to the one he remembered Glenda had shown him and even demonstrated in his presence.

“Have you been game to use it yet?”

“No,” she replied with a chuckle. “I’m still fearful I will react badly because of the experience with *‘you know who’*. I need you present to calm me. To make it feel like an act of love, not sexual abuse.”

“Now? Or tonight?” he inquired.

“Now,” she said getting to her feet. “Down by the stream. I want to make us both deliriously happy. Experience a special joy that will linger on in our lives. Bring the rug, my towel, the cushion for my head, and that tube of lubricant.”

Once they were partly undressed and comfortably settled, Andrew's misery dissipated. He squeezed out some lubricant and rubbed it around Connie's vulva lips, letting her accept his index finger for the first time. He took it slowly, waiting till the love juice was oozing from her vagina, then cautiously touching her clitoris and searching for the G-spot.

"Is that okay?" he asked politely as Connie began to writhe with joy.

"Now, the vibrator," he continued. "I'll inch it in slowly at first till you're accustomed to the feel of it."

Connie was moaning quietly, her body responding to the delights. It was the pleasure she had denied herself for ten years. It was time for a champagne treat. When Andrew hit the switch the vibrations fired throughout her vagina, her abdomen, her whole entranced being. She had entered into an orgasmic feast where her vagina had become her whole universe. She was nothing else but pussy. There were no words, only moan after moan from her quivering lips, as the vibrator touched sensitive spot after sensitive spot. The lorikeets' exuberance, loud as it was from hundreds of birds drunk on nectar, could not match Connie's explosive shrieks. It had become imperative that she thrust forward to demand more and more of the thrills.

Andrew too was losing control, joining in with groan upon groan, as his engorged shaft exploded into his jocks. Yet he let it be a minor disruption, just enough for him to pause and ease the vibrator out past her swollen labia, thinking it was probably enough for her first time.

Connie had other desires. She pulled her legs right back into the oyster position exposing herself fully for Andrew and managed the words, “Your turn, my love.”

He took the hint and pressed lips to lips to kiss and taste. Connie thrust her pubes at him and moaned louder and louder as his tongue went searching and found her clitoris. The air filled with the giant ‘aah’ upon ‘aah’ of a stupendous orgasm, the sound echoing through the hills, silencing the lorikeets that took off in fright. Connie was not frightened, this was her moment, the one she had most waited for, crying, crying…Streuth! …Strewth! …Stroo…ooth! …into the Salvator Rosa air, and Andrew, equally in orgasmic joy, obliged by drinking her juices and feasting on the wonder of cunnilingus…until exhaustion took over, and they rolled together into the cool water of the stream—entwined, spent, and content.